DEBT OF VENGEANCE

To: Doris

It was a pleasure to meet you.

I hope you enjoy the book

Thanks

DEBT OF VENGEANCE

Zane Sterling

LANGDON STREET PRESS

Langdon Street Press
212 3rd Avenue North, Suite 290
Minneapolis, MN 55401
612.455.2293
www.langdonstreetpress.com

ISBN - 978-1-934938-71-3
ISBN - 1-934938-71-8
LCCN - 2009931611

Book sales for North America and international:
Itasca Books, 5120 Cedar Lake Road
Minneapolis, MN 55416
Phone: 952.345.4488 (toll free 1.800.901.3480)
Fax: 952.920.0541; email to orders@itascabooks.com

Cover Design by Alan Pranke
Typeset by Peggy LeTrent

Printed in the United States of America

Acknowledgment

I would like to thank all my friends and family who have made the publishing of *Debt of Vengeance* possible. The list is too long to mention each of you individually, but nonetheless, you all have my humblest and sincerest thanks. I would like to say a special thanks to my two sons, Clayton and Quaid, my greatest inspirations.

Zane Sterling

FOREWORD

What is it that makes a man what he is? Are there many factors that blend together over one's years that determine the direction of our lives? Or, is it possible that one substantial event overrides all? Perhaps it is fate or a predetermined destiny. Maybe our lives are scripted much like a story in a book, whereas we have no voice but are merely ink on a page.

As I sit in a fading sunlight that is filtered by steel bars, listening to the banging of a hammer and the grating of a saw, I think of these things. Perhaps thinking of such things is merely a waste of time. Because tomorrow, when the sun once again rises above the eastern horizon, none of it will make a difference. The result will be the same ... and I suppose in the end the result is all that really matters.

Six years ago, with the encouragement of my mother, I began keeping a diary. I was a gangly sixteen-year-old boy at that time. The diary was something

I did not write in every day, but mostly when I felt something of significance had happened. To a young boy of sixteen, with an unquenchable thirst for life and enough goals and dreams for two lifetimes, something significant happens nearly every day. That is how it was for me, anyway.

As I followed a team of mules, holding on to the smooth wooden handles of a plow that sank deep in the heavy, black soil, my mind was elsewhere. It was far, far away from that one-hundred and sixty-acre cotton farm in Tennessee. Mostly it was in Texas working as a cowboy, or seeking my fortune in the gold and silver towns of Tombstone, Arizona, or Virginia City, Nevada. Places I had heard of but of course had never seen.

My work suffered as much from this kind of thinking, as my rows were seldom straight. I think it was reasons like this that my declaration of leaving home came as no surprise to my father. It was something that was probably known to him, even before I myself knew.

Two weeks following my eighteenth birthday, I stood hat in hand in front of my parents. I will never forget that day, as a steady drizzle softly fell from a solemn, gray sky. Nor will I ever forget the deep sadness that I saw in my mother's eyes. It is a memory that painfully tugs at my heart to this day. I am sure my father felt the same way, to a certain extent. But I suppose he also felt the pride that a man has for a son whose independence and determination drive him to reach for the stars. Even if the stars he grasps for are far different from his own.

Sadie, my black mare, stood quietly at my side. My saddlebags, containing all of my earthly belongings, were barely half-full. The elbows of my denim coat were worn thin, as were the knees and seat of my homespun britches. The felt hat that I wore was my father's. It was heavily stained with the dirt and sweat of an honest man making an honest living.

I saw a faint quiver in my father's chin as he reached out and placed his work-hardened hands on my shoulders. "Son, I reckon, I ain't got much to say," he said as he slowly nodded his head. "I suppose all I have to really give ya' is the Tucker family name. Carry it proudly as we have."

A lump formed in my throat that hardly allowed me to speak. "I will," I said. "I promise ya', I will."

My mother began sobbing as we clasped our arms around each other. Neither of us knew when or if we would ever again have this opportunity to feel the comfort of each other's arms. As I leaned down to kiss her, I felt her warm tears against my face. "I'll be fine, Mama," I said reassuringly. "Don't you worry none about me. I'll be fine."

She could only nod as she struggled to force a teary smile.

Mounting my horse, I slowly rode away from that Tennessee farm, disappearing into the heavy, gray clouds that hugged the gently, rolling hills. Drops of water spilled from the brim of my hat as I turned and looked over my shoulder one last time. Turning back around, I squeezed my horse into a trot as tears stung my eyes.

Over the course of the next four years, I was able to mark many things from that list of dreams that I had so long compiled in my mind. I punched cattle down in South Texas on the Three-Bar, where over time I developed the reputation of a good, dependable hand. Not a top hand, as my roping was on the lacking side, but the kind of man, as the saying goes, to ride the river with. I have tasted the dust of the Chisholm Trail, as we pushed three thousand head of longhorns to Dodge City, Kansas. Along the way, we endured stampedes and encounters with herd-cutters as well as renegade Indians.

I saw, first hand, the wrath of Mother Nature as an angry, storm-swollen Red River reared its ugly head. Not only did the muddy water claim the lives of seventy-five head of cattle, but also the life of Jimmy Reed, a young man whom I considered a dear friend. I felt the pain and anguish of his parents as I had the self-imposed responsibility of relaying the news of that sad and tragic day.

I came to know the feeling of seeing a gold nugget sparkle in my pan as I squatted in the edge of the South Fork of the Yuba River in California. That cold, clear water tumbled its way past me over a riverbed of large, majestic boulders, carving a deep path through the magnificent and daunting Sierras. I was like most prospectors; my ambition of striking it rich never came to fruition. However, with a lot of hard, backbreaking work, I was able to save a good grubstake. From what I had witnessed, I considered that more fortunate than many.

I have felt the cold, crisp air of the Rockies drawn deep into my lungs after a passing snowstorm, and I have witnessed the awe-inspiring beauty of cactus flowering in the scorching heat of the Arizona desert. I have stood next to lakes and rivers where water seemed to be an unlimited quantity, only to be reminded of its scarcity in far West Texas.

I have witnessed the birth of a young boy in the back bayous of Louisiana, as well as the senseless killing of a man named Joe Cagle in Deadwood, South Dakota. One crying out for their first breath, the other drawing his last as his blood seeped from a bullet hole, only to be absorbed by sawdust on a filthy saloon floor.

I have known remarkable men and women who came together in an earnest and caring manner to survive hardship and adversity to improve their communities and make them grow stronger, while others allowed their greed to dictate the tearing apart of areas such as Lincoln County, New Mexico.

I, like most wandering men, have done many things, some of which I am not proud. I know all too well the morning taste of whiskey on my breath after a long night of drinking, or the firm feel of cards in my hands and the softness of a bought woman lying next to me.

On a beautiful spring morning in 1882, outside the small New Mexico town of Clear Fork, my life would change forever.

My name is Chance Tucker ... and this is my story.

CHAPTER 1

The small town of Tascosa sat in the northwestern edge of the Texas panhandle. It was not a big place by any standards, but it was a town that carried the well-earned reputation of leaning toward the side of wild and woolly. I guess in that regard it was similar to some of the mustangs I had broke over the years; it was a little hard to curry below the knees.

My partner and friend, Tig Jones, rode next to me. Tig was two years my junior, having turned twenty years old the previous week. While he had a heart as big as the palm-leafed hat he wore, and the honesty of an ordained Baptist preacher, he also carried the well-earned reputation of making hasty and impulsive decisions at times. However, no truer friend have I ever known. Much like myself, he had left his family's East Texas farm three years prior with the intent of becoming a cowboy. A life he perceived as one of freedom and independence and of being his own man, never having

7

to answer to anyone. I have come to believe that most men are bound by their own limitations.

Wearing two weeks worth of West Texas dust on our clothes and the weariness of a long trail weighing on our shoulders, we were not overly concerned with the reputation of the town. Our only concerns were a bath, a shot of whiskey or two, and a well-deserved rest for our horses. We turned our fatigued mounts down the narrow dusty street. The majority of the buildings were low-roofed adobes. Scant others were made of wood planking that had grayed over the passage of time, never given the proper dignity nor respectfulness of a coat of paint.

It was sweltering hot. A small number of puffy, cotton ball type clouds drifted aimlessly in the otherwise empty sky, giving only moments of relief as the coolness of their shadows quickly swept across the summer-cured grass.

"Do ya' remember the last time we was here?" Tig asked as he glanced over at me.

"Yeah, I remember," I replied.

"We had a pretty good time then, didn't we?"

I shook my head as I shot him a skeptical glance. "You must remember different than I do. The best I remember you got your ass whooped right there in that saloon," I said as I pointed a finger toward a low-slung adobe building called *Dirty Pete's*.

Tig furrowed his brow as we walked our horses past the saloon and headed toward the town's public watering trough. "Yeah, I reckon I did," he finally conceded. "I had plum forgot about that. Anyway, that was better than two years ago. I bet it would be different now."

"You got to be kiddin' me," I replied as we stepped from our saddles and allowed our horses to drink from the wooden trough. "I don't reckon it would be different at all."

"What do ya' mean?" he retorted. "Hell, I'm older and stronger now. Plus," he threw in for good measure, "I was drunk then. Yep, the way I see it, it would be a dead-gut-cinch."

Tig had a gift, if you want to call it that, of coming up with creative words or phrases that I had come to figure out usually didn't mean a dang thing. Nevertheless, it seemed to keep him amused, and I guess overall it did me as well.

"I don't think it would've mattered. That man was one of the biggest, toughest men I've ever seen anywhere in my life. What was his name? Oh yeah, I remember, Jack Morgan. They called him the gentle giant. That was a bunch of bull," I added. "When you broke that chair over his back there wasn't nothin' gentle about him at all."

Tig chuckled at the memory. The windmill, in need of a good greasing, creaked and groaned as the wooden-blades whirled in the hot Texas breeze.

After the horses had drank their fill we dipped our heads into the cool water. Socking our hats down over our dripping, wet hair, we swung back into our saddles and rode the half block before dismounting in front of *Dirty Pete's*.

Tascosa was as much a meeting place for business deals as it was a town. Its lifeline was being strategically located between the enormous ranches that swallowed a substantial part of Texas and half of New Mexico. It was overall a lawless place where the reputable and disreputable were equally accepted at face value. No questions asked. Even though it was the middle of the week and the middle of the day, horses were lined up shoulder-to-shoulder, standing hipshot in front of the saloon.

Looping our reins over the hitch rail, I followed Tig through the batwing doors of *Dirty Pete's*.

We had no more than stepped inside when Tig called out, "Well, I'll be go to hell! Look who's here!"

Stepping out from behind Tig, I saw Jack Morgan standing at the crowded bar. He was easy to spot as he stood a full head above the other men bellied to the bar. His shoulders were as broad as a barn door and the beer mug he held was all but covered up by his ham-sized hands.

Morgan, the gentle giant, turned at the remark, as did everyone else in the bar. His eyes quickly locked on Tig.

"You remember me, big man?" Tig smirked as he began unhitching his gun belt.

"Come on, Tig," I urged. "We don't want no

trouble. Let's just get us a drink like we said we was gonna do and go on about our business."

Tig shrugged me off as he handed me his rigging. All eyes were on him as he confidently strode over to Jack Morgan.

"Oh, hell," I mumbled under my breath.

Although Tig stood about five-eleven or so and weighed around a hundred and eighty pounds, he looked like a dwarf as he stood in front of Morgan. "The last time I was here, I was drunk," Tig smirked. "This time I ain't. Not yet anyways."

The men at the bar quickly scattered, leaving a large circle around the two men. Jack Morgan smiled but I could tell there was no humor in the action. "Maybe you ought to just have yourself a warm glass of milk, son. I'm sure it would be a lot better for your health. The same as it would've been the last time you was here," he added.

As Morgan started to turn back toward the bar, Tig swung a haymaker that started from somewhere south down around Del Rio. The punch landed with a solid thud on the side of Morgan's right ear. Morgan, unfazed by the blow, quickly turned. I could tell the gentleness had once again dissipated into the thin layer of gray smoke that clung to the low ceiling in the crowded saloon.

Tig was bobbing and weaving, sticking and moving, lashing out with lefts and rights. Morgan, after taking several of the punches, threw a straight right hand of his own. Tig bobbed when he should have weaved. Morgan's gigantic fist landed flush on Tig's jaw with a crack that could have been heard from across the street. Tig's eyes rolled to the back of his head as he folded up like a cheap accordion and crumpled to the floor.

Morgan stood triumphantly over Tig before his eyes slowly turned toward me. "Do you want some of that? Or are you smarter than your friend here?" he asked as he motioned toward Tig.

Now, I always did consider myself a mite smarter than Tig in some regards and deep down I knew that I really didn't care to have a helping of what he just dished out to Tig. However, something about the sarcasm in Jack Morgan's remarks just sort of soured in the pit of my stomach.

Glancing down at my partner, I dropped Tig's gun belt to the sawdust-covered floor and quickly tore into the big man. Both of my fists were firing like the hind feet of a bee-stung mule. Trying to stay away from the powerful swings of Morgan's heavily muscled arms and knotted fists, I deftly shot a left jab to his chin followed by a straight right hand that landed solid and opened a deep gash over his left eye. Morgan momentarily staggered from the blow as the blood from the cut began flowing into his eye, blurring his vision. Sensing my opportunity, I quickly moved in to finish him off.

The next thing I knew I was sputtering for my breath as I lay sprawled out in the dusty street in front of the saloon. Tig lay moaning next to me. A man was standing over us holding an empty water pail. The large crowd from the bar had gathered outside around us, their amusement was easy to see on their faces. Painfully getting my legs underneath me, my head spinning like the squeaky blades of the windmill, I unsteadily stood up. Reaching down, I helped Tig struggle to his feet. His palm-leaf hat was on backwards, the crown smashed as flat as a pancake. His gun belt lay in the street next to him.

"I sure 'nuf thought you boys had ol' Jack," the man holding the pail quipped. "Well, until the fight started that is." With that remark, a round of laughter rippled through the amused crowd.

I gathered up Tig's gun belt before we staggered over to our horses and climbed clumsily into our saddles. Hanging on to our saddle horns for balance, we began to leave town at a slow painful walk. Passing the group of men in front of *Dirty Pete's* would normally have been extremely embarrassing, but the pain we were in more than overrode any humiliation. Neither one of us spoke as I sat stewing in anger at Tig for putting us in that uncalled-for situation.

We had not gone more than a couple of miles from town when a lone rider who had been following us pulled abreast. As our horses walked along, I saw the man glancing over at us as he took in our battered condition. Casually he retrieved the makings from his shirt pocket and rolled a smoke. "I don't reckon that was the smartest thing I ever saw done," he drawled, with a hint of a smile on his face. "But I have to admit it took more than a bucketful of sand."

I looked over at the man but not for long, as it was too painful to turn my head that far. I noticed in the brief glance that he was a rather large, rawboned man, his skin bronzed and weathered by the Texas sun. His eyes were a cool gray, matching the color of his drooping mustache. The horse he rode was coal black, standing sixteen hands or better, equaling the man's size.

I didn't recall seeing him in Dirty Pete's but everything went to hell-in-a-hand basket so quick, I didn't know that I would have.

Reaching up, I winced as I gingerly touched my hand to my swollen face. I could tell, from my pinched vision, one eye was completely shut and the other reduced to a mere slit. My lips were puffed out to the point I thought they might burst with the slightest touch.

"Yep," he chided as he shook his head, "you boys look pretty bad. You know, of all the men that have ever taken on Jack Morgan, I've never seen or even heard of the same man trying it twice like your partner there did."

Out of the corner of my one good eye, if ya' want to call it that, I could see Tig riding slump-shouldered, his chin resting on his chest. I knew he was in some kind of hurt when he didn't even bother replying to the remark.

"My name is John McCandle," the man offered.

"I'm Chance Tucker," I said. "My brilliant partner over here is Tig Jones."

"I'm staying up the ways just a few miles," he said. "Why don't you boys come by my place and I'll see if we can get ya'll fixed up a bit?"

I nodded, not even trying to look over again. "Mister, I believe we'll take ya' up on that offer."

When we turned into the yard of the small weathered house, I couldn't tell if it was getting dark or if my other eye was swelling shut. I sure hoped it was getting dark. Soon as we pulled our horses to a halt in front of the house, an aging, bowlegged cowhand quickly came shuffling over to us from a nearby bunkhouse. His face wrinkled at the sight of us, similar to the expression you would expect of someone staring at the catastrophic results of a train wreck.

"Roy, help me get these two fellows inside," John McCandle said as he stepped down from the big black. "And then turn their horses in the corral with some hay and a bait of oats."

"Yes, sir," the cowboy replied as he hurried to Tig's side.

I unsteadily slid out of the saddle, leaning against my mare, Sadie, for support. I heard Tig muttering under his breath as Roy helped him down from his horse.

With help, we entered the sparsely furnished house and sat down around a small table. Roy immediately shambled through the door to tend the stock as John McCandle began heating a pot of water on a cook stove.

Sitting across the table from Tig was the first opportunity I had to look squarely at his face. His jaw was grossly swollen and his chin was beginning to turn black and blue. "Dead-gut cinch, huh? You look like warmed-over death," I mumbled as I shook my head.

Tig looked up slowly. "I don't see how you could tell, looking through those eyes," he slurred before grimacing from the pain of moving his jaw. I started to counter the snide remark but found it required too much effort to do so.

When the water began boiling on the stove, McCandle sat the pot between us on the table, along with a couple of rags. "Here," he said as he dipped the rags into the hot water and squeezed them out. "See if these help any."

Reaching out, I took one of the rags from him and gently pressed it to my face. The water was hot, but it felt good and soothing.

Later that evening, McCandle cooked up a batch of soup. Thinking ahead, he cut the pieces of meat into small bites. I noticed John and Roy watching Tig and I out of the corner of their eyes as we attempted to eat. It was a little painful to chew but it tasted good. Tig, unable to chew at all, was reduced to drinking the broth, leaving the tiny pieces of meat sitting in the bottom of the otherwise empty bowl. After several cups of coffee, Tig and I rolled our bedrolls out on the bunkhouse floor. With a lot of moaning and groaning, we painfully crawled on top of our blankets and slept hard.

The next several days we didn't move around much, we mostly sat around licking our wounds and trying to reconfigure what was left of our pride. I noticed John McCandle was gone the majority of the time. Most of the time he was gone during the day, however on several occasions he did not return until well into the night or even the following morning.

By the end of the week, we were both feeling a little better and spent more time sitting in the shade of the covered front porch. During that time, we got to know Roy pretty well, as he was an easy talker. The elder cowboy said he rode for the Cross-T Ranch. Preferring the solitude of the open prairie to the boisterousness of young cowboys, he had spent the better part of the last five years here on the remote north side of their range.

John McCandle, on the other hand, was friendly enough but tight-lipped when it came to the reason for him being here on this ranch. Even Roy, who had worked on the Cross-T for most of ten years, was kept out of the loop when it came to the big man who rode the big black horse.

One evening as Roy, Tig and I sat on the porch watching the shadows lengthen as the sun sat behind us, McCandle rode into the yard. After un-tacking his horse and turning him into the corral, he walked over and pulled up a chair next to us on the porch.

"I don't know if it will make you boys feel any better or not," he said dryly, "but I saw Jack Morgan today. Now don't get me wrong on this, 'cause he didn't look near as bad as you two, but it was plain to see by the bruising and scrapes on his face there was no doubt he knew he'd been in a pretty good scrap."

The news didn't really make me feel any better as I was trying to put the whole sordid debacle out of my mind. But, I could tell by the look on Tig's face that he somehow found some pittance of solace in the fact. I felt myself growing irritated at him once again.

"Well, I'll tell ya' one thing," Tig remarked through a still tender jaw, "remember that day ya' said ya' had never seen anybody take on Jack Morgan twice?"

McCandle nodded his head.

"Well, you can bet your bottom dollar, you dang sure ain't gonna see a third time. Not from me ya' ain't."

A grin showed behind McCandle's drooping mustache. "Well, maybe it turned out to be a good thing then. Maybe ol' Jack beat some sense into ya'."

Tig grinned at the comment. Rubbing his still slightly swollen jaw, he said, "I reckon he done that. As much sense as I'm probably ever gonna have in this life anyways."

A coyote trotted through the tall, brown grass only a stone's throw from the porch, its nose to the ground. Catching our scent, it paused and gave us a dismissing glance, before continuing on its way. "So, Chance, where are you boys headed?" McCandle asked as he rolled a cigarette.

"I don't know for sure. Maybe we'll head into New Mexico," I replied. "We need to find us a ridin' job somewhere."

John McCandle sat in silence as his gray eyes studied the distance. "Whoever ya' go to work for make sure they're on the up and up," he said with a very serious look on his face. "There's plenty of 'em in that part of the country that ain't. And I guarantee ya' one of these days it will catch up with 'em and there will be hell to pay. If a fellar dances with the devil long enough, eventually he has to pay the fiddler. And when that time comes it will be one hell of a steep price." After pausing again, he added. "Ya'll are good young men and I sure don't want to see ya' get caught in the middle of somethin' ya' can't get out of."

The conversation struck me a little odd. I knew John McCandle was giving us some good, solid advice but there seemed to be more to it. There seemed to be a much deeper meaning than what rippled on the surface. I had a strong feeling the secretive life he led somehow made him privy to information most men would not normally possess.

The following morning Tig and I rode out with

the rising of another fiery sun. Our horses were rested and fresh and Sadie stepped out in a lively, ground-covering trot. The day had a feel of one that would be hot and dry.

We left behind us in the distance the golden summer-cured grass of the Texas panhandle and the town of Tascosa. One thing we carried with us for a while longer was the greenish-yellow bruising on our faces.

CHAPTER 2

July was hot. Angling our way down toward Fort Sumner, New Mexico, we found no relief from the parched winds and the blistering heat.

"I'm startin' to think we should've maybe went up to Colorado," Tig said as he removed his large-brimmed hat and mopped sweat from the band with his kerchief. "At least it's a little cooler up that way."

"Yeah, I reckon it would be," I said as I swatted a pestering horsefly away from my mare. "But by the time we got up there it wouldn't be cool, it would be fall and colder than a well digger's ass."

Tig nodded as we trudged along through the dusty heat. "Yeah, that's probably right. And being cold is one thing I hate."

We rode in silence awhile before Tig looked over at me. "What do ya' reckon Mister McCandle was doing back there in Tascosa?"

"I don't know," I said as I unhooked my canteen

from my saddle horn and took a long drink. "I've been thinking about it a lot but I ain't figgered it out yet."

"You don't think he was rustlin' cattle or horses, do ya'?"

I shook my head. "Naw, I don't think so. He didn't seem the type."

"He sure wasn't cowboy'n," Tig stated. "Did ya' notice he wasn't even carryin' a rope on his saddle?"

"Yeah, I did notice that."

"All I know," Tig said, "is he sure kept odd hours."

"The only thing I can figger, that makes any sense, is maybe he's some sort of range detective," I said. "Or somethin' like that."

"You might be right," Tig nodded. "I hadn't thought of that. But now that ya' mention it that does makes sense, though."

"That's my guess," I shrugged.

Tig shook his head. "He was a nice enough fella, but I don't reckon I would want him on my trail. He has a look of a man that could get mighty serious if he had a callin' to."

"Yeah, I think so too. I'm sure, if it ever came down to it, we'd rather have him on our side than against us."

Nearing sunset we rode our horses into a shallow, brush-lined draw and made camp for the night. A trickle of water from the head of the draw gathered to form a small pool. After the horses drank their fill there was just enough water left for Tig and me to take a spit-bath.

We staked the horses out on a patch of grass a little farther down the ravine but still within sight. With a small fire going and the coffee just beginning to boil, a voice called from the night. "Hallo the camp."

I instantly pulled my pistol and backed into the shadows, as did Tig. "Come on in, Mister" I called out. "Just keep your hands where we can see 'em."

Within minutes, a lone rider rode into the edge of the firelight. He was a young man somewhere around our age. His horse had been ridden hard, its coat glistening with a foamy sweat. Tethered behind him was a string of three more horses. From what I could tell in the firelight, they all seemed to be of excellent flesh.

We walked from the shadows as the man slid down from his horse with an easy grace. "I'm by myself boys," he said as he flashed a bucktoothed smile. "I was just looking for a bite to eat and a cup of coffee if ya' boys have any extra to spare."

"We have enough," I said as I returned my pistol to its holster.

"I'll just stake my horses out down the draw a ways."

Before he turned to tend to his horses, he glanced at the near empty pool where the water had been. "There's usually a little water here," he stated.

"There was when we first got here," Tig said.

"Our horses drank it all up."

"That's all right. It'll fill up again within a couple of hours. It always does."

As he walked down the draw, I sat down. But not before I again pulled my pistol and laid it next to my leg, out of sight. For some reason that I couldn't put my finger on, I felt a little uneasy. The man seemed cordial enough, but there's usually some kind of reason for a man to ride a horse as hard as his had been ridden. Tig didn't seem concerned as he busied himself with skinning a jackrabbit he had shot earlier in the afternoon.

When the man returned, I said, "Help yourself to the coffee. There's an extra cup next to the pot."

"Much obliged," he said. Filling his cup, he sat down across the fire from me. "My name's William."

"I'm Chance and that's Tig."

"Nice to meet you boys."

"I hope you ain't too picky about the vittles. All we got is a half-starved jackrabbit."

"That'll do just fine," he said as he tentatively took a sip of the steaming coffee. "When ya' haven't eaten in a couple of days a man sure can't go around being picky. You know the old saying, beggars can't be choosey."

I studied him as he drank his coffee. He was of average height but thinly built with narrow shoulders. His front teeth were unusually large compared to the rest of his features. He had a layer of trail dust on his clothes but his tied-down gun was clean as a whistle.

Tig threw the rabbit into a greased skillet and grabbed himself a cup of coffee before sitting down. "That sure looked like some nice horses you was leadin'."

"Yep, they sure are. You fellas interested in buying 'em?" he asked. "I really need to sell 'em."

"Naw. I reckon we ain't got much need for horses, other than the ones we got," I said.

"I'll sell 'em cheap," he urged. "I need to raise a little money, quick."

"How much?" Tig asked.

"Oh, I don't know. How about twenty-five a head?"

I wrinkled my brow as I heard the price. I instantly got a little more suspicious. In ranching country you couldn't hardly buy a broken-down plow horse for that kind of money. Even though I had only caught a quick look at the horses, I had no doubt those horses were quality mounts. I figured they would be worth somewhere between seventy-five and a hundred dollars if they were worth a penny.

Tig immediately scrambled to his feet. "Twenty-five dollars," he exclaimed. "For that price we might be interested."

"That's a good price all right," I stated flatly "But we ain't interested."

Spinning on his heels, Tig started to protest before catching the hard look in my eyes. "Yeah, I guess my partner's right. We really ain't got much use for 'em.."

The man's eyes immediately went to me as we stared at each other across the fire. His light blue eyes had turned frosty cold before they once again softened as a grin crossed his narrow face. "All right," he conceded. "No harm in asking."

"Nope, no harm at all," I agreed.

I could tell an anxiousness was riding him like the devil as he impatiently waited for the rabbit to cook. More than once, he went to check on his horses. After the first time, I got the feeling he wasn't just checking on his horses, but was listening for sounds in the night. And I had a dubious feeling the sounds he was listening for were not normal sounds, but rather for the sound of someone. I found comfort in the feel of the walnut grip of the forty-five as it rested at my fingertips.

Tig seemed completely oblivious to anything out of the ordinary. Maybe it was just me. It was possible that I was allowing my suspicions to get the best of me. But my gut told me different. I had learned the hard way over the years if I was going to err, it was going to be on the side of caution. Out in the middle of an empty land like this, a man's first mistake could very well end up being his last.

"Chow's ready," Tig called out as he began divvying up the scrawny rabbit.

"Ya'll go ahead," I said. "I'm not hungry."

Tig gave me a questioning glance.

It was then that I suspected the man who called himself William noticed my empty holster. He looked over at me with penetrating blue eyes. His eyes held on me a moment before he picked up his share of the rabbit and quickly picked it clean.

Wiping his fingers on his pants as he stood up, he said, "Well boys, I appreciate the food and the coffee but I got to go."

"You ain't rested your horses much," Tig mumbled around a spindly leg bone.

"Naw, I ain't got time," he replied. "I've got some urgent business I need to tend to."

As he started to leave, he suddenly stopped and turned back around. "Hey, Tig. Stick close to your partner here. You've got yourself a good one."

The statement put a confused look on Tig's face. "Sure," he said. "I always do."

With that, William disappeared into the night. Within a couple of minutes, we heard his horses thundering off into the blackness.

Tig shook his head as the drumming of hooves disappeared into the distance. "What do ya' reckon he meant by that?"

I shrugged my shoulders. "Ya' got me," I said as I slipped my forty-five back into its holster.

The next morning at daybreak as we were rolling our blankets, six horsemen came riding in hard and fast. Their trailing dust fogged on top of us as they pulled their horses to a halt on the edge of the draw and quickly scanned our camp. The men were hard looking, one of them wearing a badge.

The man wearing the badge spoke. "Did a fella come ridin' through here last night?"

"Yes, sir," Tig replied.

"Which way did he go?"

Tig turned to point to the northeast. "He went yonder way."

Putting spurs to their horses they left at a gallop.

As the last rider sped by, Tig called out to him. "Who is it you're chasin'?"

"William Bonney."

"Who?" Tig hollered.

The man yelled over his shoulder. "William Bonney!"

Having trouble hearing over the pounding hooves of the fleeting horses, Tig hollered again. "William who?"

"Billy the Kid!"

Out of the corner of my eye, I saw Tig's face go pale as a sickly look took hold of him.

CHAPTER 3

The price of beef was down and riding work was as hard to come by as hen's teeth. The size of our pokes was dwindling fast as the rejections at all of the ranches we came to were adding up. The prospect of finding a job seemed as bleak as the land over which we rode. I was nearing the point of admitting the decision to leave Texas had been a mistake when we topped out on a bare, windswept rise.

Below us a cowboy had a rope around the outstretched horns of a steer, trying in vain to pull it from a muddy bog. The cowboy was hollering and cussing a blue streak above the bawling of the steer. His horse strained beneath him as the lariat stretched tight enough to play a high note. The heavy red clay refused to relinquish its unyielding grip on the longhorn. I figured the young cowboy could not have been older than sixteen or maybe seventeen. However, the unlimited vocabulary of cusswords he put on display would have put most grown men that I knew to shame.

Riding down to the nearly dry creek, I said, "How about a little help?"

The young cowboy quickly glanced over at me as he continued pulling on the rope. "That'd be good," he replied as he encouraged his horse with a pop from the end of his leather reins and a few blistering words.

I immediately unthonged my lariat and sent a loop over the wide horns. As I dallied the lariat around my saddle horn, Sadie quickly leaned into the rope.

After a couple of minutes, I stopped. "Hold on a minute," I called out. "If we keep this up we're just gonna end up breakin' that steer's neck."

The cowboy reluctantly eased up on his rope. The steer was bogged down to its belly in the red mud, its nostrils flaring with the exertion.

"That's the third one this week," the cowboy spouted disgustedly as he shook his head and threw in a few expletives for good measure. "I been tellin' Mister Ross for three months we needed to clean this waterin' hole out."

"Well, it's a little late now," I said I as studied the situation.

Tig suddenly dismounted and began pulling off his boots and gun belt.

"What are ya' gonna do?" I asked.

"I'm gonna go in there and push while ya'll pull. If we don't get it unstuck it'll die in there. We can't let that happen." As he entered the bog, he immediately sank to his thighs in the gooey mud. Sloshing his way behind the steer he grabbed its tail and began twisting as we urged our horse against the ropes once again. We were about to give up when suddenly the mud released its firm grip with a loud suctioning noise. Tig, off balance, fell face-first into the red mud as we slid the steer out of the mud and onto the dry creek bank.

We quickly removed our ropes before the angry longhorn had enough energy to attack us. As we sat our horses, watching from a safe distance, the steer struggled to its feet before walking off on trembling legs. With the coast clear, Tig crawled toward the bank on his belly. He was slathered in the red muck from head to toe. He looked up at us as he pulled himself up on the bank. All we could see were the whites of his eyes.

We both began laughing as Tig stood up and attempted to spit the mud from his mouth. "Now what am I supposed to do?" he asked as he longingly looked at the shallow pool of water outlined by the wide ring of mud. "I sure as hell can't go in there to wash off."

The young cowboy quickly grabbed his canteen from his saddle. "This probably ain't gonna help much. But maybe it will help some."

Slowly dribbling the water in Tig's outstretched hands. He said, "I'm J.C. Jenkins, but everybody just calls me Boots."

"I'm Chance Tucker. My muddy partner here is Tig Jones."

31

"It's sure nice to meet you fellas," the young cowboy replied. "I sure 'nough appreciate your help. I was fixin' to pull my rifle and remedy the situation. Maybe if there was a dead steer in the waterin' hole, Mister Ross would send me some help so we could clean this mud bog out."

After Tig got his hands somewhat clean, he began working on his face. When all of our canteens were empty, Tig did not look much better as his face and clothes were streaked with rivulets of mud.

"There's a creek with some pretty clean water in it a couple of miles from here," Boots suggested as he shrugged his shoulders. "It ain't much but it's the closest."

I picked up Tig's boots and pistol and placed them in his saddlebags as Tig gingerly walked to his horse in bare feet.

As we rode, the hot sun quickly began baking the mud in Tig's hair and on his clothes, turning the mud from a dark red to a light red.

"I feel like I'm being cooked," Tig spewed as he continually pealed the dried mud off as we rode. "I just thought it was hot before. That reminds me, Chance, do you remember that girl up in Denver at the Bucket saloon that I run around with for a few days when we was there last year?"

I shrugged my shoulder. "I don't know. Which one?"

"I can't remember her name. The real fat one."

I grinned. "Yeah, her name was Bertha or Belle or something like that."

"Yeah, that's her," Tig said through a grin. "I heard she went up to Dakota or somewhere up yonder and was living with a trapper. And they said one day while he was off runnin' his traps she had one of them hot spells like women sometimes get and burned the whole damn cabin down."

Boots and I started laughing. Tig was hoorawing and slapping his leg so hard the mud was falling off in chunks. Turning to look over my shoulder, I could see a steady trail of dirt clods marking the path of Tig's horse.

The young cowboy had been correct when he said the creek wasn't much. When we rode up to its banks, Tig looked very disappointed. The shallow water was maybe a foot deep with a green skim of slimy moss fermenting on top.

"Ain't there any clean water in this Godforsaken place?" Tig complained as he began removing his clothes.

"Naw, not much," Boots replied. "Not around here there ain't, not this time of year. Hell, you're just lucky ya' got here when ya' did. By next week, unless we get some rain, there might not be none at all."

"Well, this is just dandy," Tig spouted as he waded buck-naked into the shin-deep water. Frogs quickly scattered into the protection of the murky water. "Yeah, and just for the record, I do consider myself to be real lucky just like ya' said."

I started to get the feeling that Tig was growing a little red under the collar at the whole situation and I was pretty sure it wasn't just the color of the mud that was stuck on his neck. Taking my boots off and rolling my pants legs up, I grabbed a long stick and began scraping the layer of moss off the top. After only a couple of minutes, I pretty well had the shallow pool cleared. As Tig continued to try to get the dried mud off his skin and out of his hair, I took his clothes and began rinsing them out as best as I could.

"Say, you fellas ain't huntin' a job are ya?" Boots asked as he flung a rock at a small frog setting next to the bank.

Tig and I both turned at the question. "Yeah, we are," I replied. "You know where we can get one?"

"Yeah, my partner up and quit last week," he said. "The Box-T ranch headquarters is about fifteen miles west of here."

"How are they to work for?" I asked.

Boots shrugged his shoulders. "I guess they're all right. To be honest ya' don't see 'em much. They send a fellar out once a month to pay ya' if you're still here."

"That's sounds like a pretty good job to me," Tig said as he tiptoed out of the green water.

"The Ross's don't pay as well as the other ranches around, but it's mainly a ridin' job. There ain't no fence buildin' and as you can see, there sure as hell ain't no cleanin' out waterin' holes. It's mostly just keepin' the cattle from strayin' off where they ain't supposed to be and keeping cattle from surrounding ranches off Mister Ross's grass. Other than that it's just brandin' a few calves when they hit the ground, or the ones that got missed during the spring roundup."

I hung Tig's clothes up to dry in the scrawny branches of a mesquite tree as he retrieved his only other clothes from his saddlebags. They were not clean, but they were definitely cleaner than the ones hanging from the thorny branches of the tree.

As Tig stamped his feet into his boots, he asked, "Ya' reckon they'll hire both of us?"

Boots nodded. "Yep, I reckon so."

"What makes ya' so sure?" Tig asked. "With your partner quittin' it sounds like they may only need to hire one hand."

"Naw, two," Boots remarked confidently.

"How ya' figger?" Tig quizzed.

The young cowboy swung into his saddle and turned his horse. "Cause I just quit too."

"What?"

"They paid off this morning and I don't reckon I need anymore of this," he said as he put spurs to the horse and began loping away.

"So what are we supposed to tell 'em about you?" I called out.

"I don't much care," he hollered over his shoulder. "You can tell 'em I said they can all go straight …"

His words faded into the windy distance. However, I pretty much got the gist of his meaning.

"So, what do ya' think?

I shrugged my shoulders as we both stood watching the young cowboy disappear into the prairie. "It sounds like we might have a pretty good shot at findin' some payin' work."

"It sort of looks that way," Tig replied with a chuckle. "I think I could've grown to like that kid."

I gave Tig a questionable glance, knowing what he said was probably true. However, I didn't really care to think about it.

I had heard of the Box-T ranch. With a large number of cowboys often being young and shallow-rooted, as Boots appeared to be, they had tendencies to drift with the wind in the always-elusive quest for greener pastures. In their tumbleweed-like-state, they carried news of different outfits with them. Usually this information was shared over a cup of coffee in a café or more often over a beer in a saloon. It was most times slanted in its views toward the bearer and often unreliable, but it was news nonetheless.

What I did know was the ranch covered well over two-hundred-thousand acres in the far reaches of western New Mexico. I did not know for sure but I figured it was mostly undeeded land like many ranches at that time. The equation was a simple one: the men with the most cattle and the most cowboys controlled most of the land.

J.B. Ross, an ex-Union officer from the Civil War, was the man in charge of the day-to-day operations of the sprawling Box-T ranch. His son, Bert, was the foreman. A group of investors from England supplied the cattle, as well as the working capital, from what I later learned.

When we rode into the headquarters of the Box-T ranch, it was not what either of us expected. With the exception of the main house, which was exceptionally well cared for, the outbuildings were in various stages of neglect.

"I've seen squatter's shacks that were better taken care of than this place," Tig said as he eyed the weathered bunkhouse and the slightly tilting barn.

"Well, I guess that explains the condition of the waterin' holes," I replied. "But Boots said he got paid on time. I guess for right now that's a little more important to me than the rest of it."

Tig shrugged his shoulders. "Yeah, I suppose so. It just seems a little odd, that's all."

As we walked our horses toward a hitch rail in front of the main house, two men stepped out onto the porch. One was graying, much like the outbuildings on the place, his weathered face grooved by sun and wind. His stern eyes held the same friendliness as that of a rattlesnake right before he strikes the nose of a curious pup. The features of the younger man looked much the same with about thirty years of wear and tear not yet accumulated.

When the eldest of the men spoke, his voice was stiff like the heavily starched shirt he wore. "If you boys are riding the grub-line in search of a free meal you might as well stay in your saddles. I'm not running a charity for drifters."

His words bit into my hide. Most ranchers were a little more on the welcoming side, at least until they found out who you were and what you wanted. Out of the corner of my eye, I could see that Tig was as chapped as I was. Knowing Tig the way I did, I could tell he was preparing to explain a few things in his own special way, so I spoke before he had the opportunity.

"We was told that you might be in need of a couple of hands," I said.

I got the feeling from the first time I opened my mouth and the words passed over my lips in a slow southern drawl that he was not at all impressed with mine and Tig's heritage.

The man stared at us long and hard before he spoke. "Well, I reckon somebody fed you boys some tainted information. I'm J.B. Ross, I run the Box-T, and we aren't hiring. So ya' might as well put your spurs to them broomtails you're riding and keep going until you're off my range," he said as he turned toward the front door of the house. "And by the way, just in case you're wondering," he said as he stopped and again glared at us, "that's about thirty miles in any direction you look from here."

I had about all of J. B Ross's arrogance that I

needed and was about to turn my mare around when Tig spoke. "That ain't what Boots said."

With that, Ross turned back around. "What did you say?"

Tig shrugged his shoulders. "That ain't what Boots said when he quit."

Ross turned on his heels. "Quit!" he repeated. "Damn lowlife saddle tramps. Did you know anything about that, Bert?"

The younger man shook his head. "No, sir. That's news to me, Pa. I haven't heard anything about it."

"That's cause it just happened," Tig said, "right after we pulled one of your steers out of a clay bog right east of here a ways."

Ross was visibly irritated as he cursed under his breath. "Bert, do whatever you want. I don't have time for this."

"There was one other thing Boots wanted me to tell you, Mister Ross," Tig said as he pretended to rack his memory. "Now what was it?" I knew Tig was relishing in the opportunity of sticking a burr under Ross's saddle. "Oh yeah, I remember. He said to tell ya' you could go straight to hell," Tig said as he innocently shrugged his shoulders. "For the life of me I don't reckon I understand why he would say such a thing as that to you, sir."

I bit my lip trying to keep a straight face as I watched the ire swell up in J.B. Ross to the point I thought a vein on the side of his head might burst. He stood there staring at Tig with a look that could have singed the hair right off a steer. Tig just sat there on his horse, an innocuous look awash on his face. Ross, mumbling a few words that were incomprehensible, turned and went into the house and slammed the door behind him.

Bert stared at the closed door a moment before he turned his attention back to us. I could tell he was struggling with the decision of hiring us when a cowboy came riding to the front of the house, leading a saddled horse behind. "Come on Bert," the man called out. "Are we going to Clear Fork or not? You know how it is, them saloon girls are a little fresher if ya' catch 'em earlier in the day."

I got the feeling that Bert's first priorities weren't necessarily the running of the ranch, but leaned more toward self-indulgence with the ladies of the evening, or in this case, the ladies of the afternoon. Knowing that someone had to replace the two cowboys that had recently quit, or having to do the job himself, he quickly explained the job responsibilities to Tig and me. I noticed that Bert Ross put great emphasis on explaining our job was to take care of the eastern fringes of the Box-T ranch and nowhere else. Being new to the area and not knowing exactly where the unmarked boundaries were, he made it plain in no uncertain terms, that wherever there was a pool of water or a tuft of grass was Box-T range.

Judging by the apprehension on Bert's face as he swung into his saddle, I could tell he was no more impressed with Tig and I than his father had been. Nevertheless, in the end, the Box-T was in need of a couple of hands and Tig and I were in need of a job.

Bert glanced over his shoulder at us several times as he and the other cowboy loped off in the direction of Clear Fork.

"I don't know," I said, "but I don't think I'd trust Mister Ross or his son as far as I could throw 'em."

Tig nodded his agreement as we turned our horses and headed east. "Yeah, me neither. But I guess as long as the crotchety old fart's money spends the same as anyone else's that's all I give a hoot about."

As we rode along, familiarizing ourselves with the lay of the land, uncertainty nagged at me. Something about the whole situation left me with a feeling that things just did not seem to tally up quite the way they should. After a while, I dismissed the notion as foolish. After all, the Box-T was a large and successful ranch, as far as I knew, and J.B. Ross had been in charge of the substantial spread for the better part of ten years.

CHAPTER 4

I sat my horse in silence as I peered down at the tracks in front of me. There was little doubt that the ten or twelve tightly bunched cows had not drifted on their own, but had been driven. Dismounting, I carefully searched until I found what I was looking for, the tracks of two shod horses. Kneeling down, I picked up a handful of the soft dirt and let it slowly sift through my fingers. It trickled away much like the Box-T cattle had been doing the last three to four months that Tig and I had been employed here.

Removing his hat and running a sleeve across his forehead, Tig asked, "What ya' reckon we ought to do, Chance?"

Standing up, my eyes followed the tracks of the cattle. "Let's follow 'em and see where they go."

Tig hesitated. "Don't ya' think we oughta check with Mister Ross first?" When I did not answer, he continued. "After all, we really ain't supposed to be this far south."

Swinging into my saddle, I said, "I don't reckon ridin' a full day in the opposite direction so we could ask Mister Ross would do much good. It would be a little late by then."

Tig furrowed his brow in thought.

My pa taught me when I was a young boy that if ya' take a man's money, ya' give him an honest days work. Therefore, that is what I did. Squeezing my horse into a trot, I headed south following the tracks. Tig quickly caught up.

The trail was a straight one, the stride of the cattle was short, giving credence to the fact that the rustlers were in no hurry as they evidently felt they were in no danger of being discovered. I found this odd that cattle thieves, with the threat of feeling the roughness of a hemp rope around their necks, rode as if they were going to a church social.

Crossing Alder Creek, I noticed the cows had been allowed to water, for the shallow stream stood heavily trampled and muddied. An uneasiness came over me as the whole situation had a smell of more wrong than right.

Several hours before sundown, Tig pulled his horse to a stop. Leaning down from his saddle, he said, "It looks like we're gettin' close."

I watched as he dismounted and buried the toe of his boot into a pile of cow manure. "Yep, that's fresh alright," he said as he picked up a stick and began trying to scrape the still-warm dung from his boot.

I grinned at the spectacle. "Maybe ya' should of just poked it with the stick to begin with?"

"Yeah, I suppose that would've made a little more sense," he chuckled as he continued the scraping.

Riding a short ways farther, the land began to break into numerous small arroyos that funneled into a rugged series of deep canyons known as Hell's Gate. I had never been here before but I had heard talk of men who had. According to them, it was a maze of mostly dead ends and box canyons with sheer rock walls climbing to a thousand feet or more. They say if a man does not know the trails or gets lost, he could wander aimlessly for days or even weeks trying to find his way out.

The trail of the cattle led directly into one of the arroyos.

Pulling my horse to a stop at the head of the arroyo, I took in the daunting beauty of the precarious canyons. The canyons were a good two miles across, and from east to west stretched as far as the eye could see. As dusk neared and the coolness of a high-desert evening closed in, a purple hue hovered over the rugged gorge.

"I don't know," I said, shaking my head as I turned the collar of my coat up to thwart the bite of the air, "somethin' just don't feel right to me." Tig nodded.

"Why would someone stealin' cattle be takin' their time like these fellas are?" I asked.

"I don't know. It don't make much sense," he replied, "unless them cows ain't stolen."

"What do ya' mean?"

"Maybe they ain't Box-T cows. Maybe they're Rocking J's that just strayed off up here and are being driven back."

That was something I had not considered. However, the idea seemed remote for the Rocking J range lay to the south of Hell's Gate. For the cattle to have been on the north side meant they would have had to cross through the steep and winding canyons. It seemed like quite a trek for overall lazy animals.

Glancing over at the setting sun, I figured we probably had no more than thirty minutes of daylight left. Hell's Gate looked intimidating enough in the light of day; I had no intention of stumbling into it in the dark.

I was about to turn my horse when out of the corner of my eye I saw something I had not seen before. Next to the trail of the cattle, a lone horseman had ridden in from the east and sat his horse next to where we now stood. The rider never dismounted but according to the number of cigarette butts that littered the ground he had sat for a while before leaving the same way he had came. The tracks were unusually large compared to that of most cow ponies you saw in the area and the indentations they left in the ground were deep as well.

"Now who do ya' reckon that was?" I asked as I studied the tracks.

Tig shrugged his shoulders. "You got me. What do you think?"

"I don't know," I said. "But whoever he is he's a large man ridin' a big horse."

Following the edge of the arroyos about a mile to the west, we found a shallow gully surrounded by a thick stand of juniper to camp for the night.

Staking out our horses, we built a small fire, one just large enough to heat a tin of beans and a small pot of coffee. Feeling a little leery about the whole situation, after eating and pouring the last cup of coffee, we immediately extinguished the fire and moved our camp a half a mile away.

As we lay in the darkness, above us the stars shined brilliantly in the moonless sky. However, without a fire, we soon began to shiver in our light coats and thin blankets. It did not take long for the night chill to overcome its own beauty.

Tig lay staring up at the sky. "Chance, can I ask ya' somethin'?"

"Sure," I said as I snugged my blanket tighter around me.

"I know you've saved a little money, what are ya' plannin' on doing with it?"

"Well, I suppose one of these days I'd like to start a small spread of my own," I said. "Maybe find a nice girl to settle down with and raise a couple of young'uns." After I thought about it a little longer, I added, "But, I ain't in no hurry."

It was silent for a while, before Tig said, "I ain't got much money saved, but I have a little. Maybe we could go together on a place. That way we could still be partners."

I smiled in the darkness. "There ain't no one I'd rather be partners with."

"That's what I was thinkin' too," he said.

The night was long, but sleep was short. It was a relief to see the stars begin to fade as we stamped our feet into our cold boots and rolled our blankets. After saddling our horses, we rode in silence toward the arroyo where the cattle had descended into Hell's Gate. We rode cautiously as we knew not what to expect.

The sun began peaking over the eastern horizon as we drew our horses up at the mouth of the ravine. Pulling my Winchester from its scabbard, I turned toward Tig. "Well, partner, are ya' ready?"

He gave a nervous nod, his blue eyes wide and unblinking. "I reckon I'm as ready as I'll ever be," he said as he pulled his own rifle.

Touching my heels to Sadie's ribs, I led the way as we began the slow, ominous descent into the bowels of Hell.

The steep, twisting trail, at the bend of the ravine, was scarcely wide enough for a man to enter on horseback as my boots more than once scraped the rock sides. Our horses, squatting low on their haunches, carefully took one cautious step after the other, the soft sand shifting unsteadily beneath their hooves. I caught myself, more than once, holding my breath as my horse slid on the unstable surface, having to scramble to regain her footing. The rock walls along the side of the trail progressively grew taller as we slowly continued the descent into the unknown maze.

Several narrow ravines fed into the one in which we rode. They twisted and turned much like the one we were in, allowing me to see but a short distance down them. At each one, I stopped and studied the ground carefully. The sand was smooth in each of them, showing no sign of tracks.

Nudging our horses forward, we painstakingly continued single-file down the narrow funnel. Rounding a sharp bend in the trail, I abruptly pulled my horse to a stop.

"I hope that was the worst of it," Tig said, unable to see around the tight switchback in front of me.

The lower side of the trail dropped off more than a hundred feet straight down, leaving a ledge, scarcely three feet wide, hugging the sheer rock wall that now jutted fifty feet above us.

My heart was racing as I tried to compose my staggered breathing. "It ain't," I finally muttered. "It ain't even close."

The deep canyons, still hidden from the morning sun, held a coolness but I felt beads of sweat trickling down my back. Glancing over my shoulder, I knew the trail was too narrow to turn around in and too steep for the horses to back out. There was only one way to go and that was forward. Giving Sadie her head, she quickly balked at the trail, taking several quick and unsteady steps backwards. Clambering for her footing, she sent a shower of sand and gravel over the edge of the narrow path and into the chasm below us.

"What's wrong?" Tig spouted nervously as he tried to see around me.

"Just don't look down," I said, struggling to sound calm. "Whatever ya' do, don't look down."

With a squeeze of my legs, I once again encouraged my horse forward. Reluctantly, she took a short step, then another. The edge of the trail disappeared beneath the width of my horse, my outside leg dangling in space. Staring straight ahead, I continued. I could hear Tig mumbling under his breath behind me, but his words were indistinguishable.

I felt my horse trembling beneath me as we rounded another sharp bend. Much to my relief, the trail opened into a flat area fifty-foot wide. Reaching the open space, I unsteadily dismounted. Leaning against my horse for support, I quickly realized that Sadie had not been trembling all this time. It was me.

When Tig reached the opening, his face was as pale as a thin sheet of parchment paper. A stream of sweat poured down his face as he struggled to calm his breathing. "There'd better be another way out of here," he gasped as he kicked his boots free from the stirrups and shakily slid to the ground. "I ain't ever doing that again."

As we stood there trying to regain our composure, my eyes went to the ground. A knot the size of a watermelon suddenly came into the pit of my stomach. The feeling must have shown on my face.

"What?" Tig anxiously blurted out. "What the hell is it?"

I slowly shook my head as our eyes met. "There ain't no tracks here," I said. "Not a one, except our own."

Tig stared at me blankly, before his eyes suddenly darted to the ground. Bending over he frantically began searching for tracks. As desperately as he searched, if there had even been a track left by a dung beetle he certainly would have found it. Slowly straightening up, the color, which just moments ago had returned to his face, once again drained to his boots.

Handing my reins to Tig, I walked a little farther down the trail. It quickly narrowed down to only a couple of feet in width, leaving barely enough room for a man, much less a horse, to walk.

Walking back to where Tig stood with the horses, I said, "Well, as bad as I hate to say this, there ain't but one thing to do."

His expression told of someone who had just been kicked in the knee by a mule. "How could that've happened?" he stammered with a pained look. "I don't see how we could have missed 'em."

"The only thing I can figger," I said as I shook my head, "they must've turned down one of those side ravines we passed and then brushed out their tracks."

"That dang sure explains why they weren't in much of a hurry," he exclaimed. "Someone would have to be a complete fool to be down here where we are."

Glancing back toward the narrow trail, a nervous laughed crossed my lips. "Well, I guess in this particular situation that pretty well sums it up."

It took me two tries to step into the saddle, as my legs were still weak and threatened not to support my own weight. Standing up in my stirrups, I adjusted the saddle underneath me. Picking up the reins, I urged my horse back toward the constricted path. Sadie held as much reservation about leaving the comfort of the opening as Tig and I did, for she stubbornly hesitated at the idea. With some diligent prodding, she cautiously once again stepped onto the narrow ledge.

Tig followed behind. I could hear him mumbling, but I could not tell if he was praying or cussing. I finally figured out it was both. He was praying and just adding a little more emphasis to certain parts that he evidently deemed more pertinent.

After crossing the ledge, we turned our horses up the narrow, sandy chute. Coming to the first offshoot ravine, I pulled my horse to a stop and dismounted. Dropping my reins, I made my way on foot down the arroyo. After following the narrow path a couple of hundred feet, I could find no evidence of cattle having come this way. Returning to my horse, I mounted and proceeded to the next one. This one was different. Rounding the first bend in the trail, there it was plain as day, the tracks of the cattle as well as the two horses.

Walking back to my horse, I said, "This is it. I should've thought about looking down 'em in the first place. I just didn't figger on 'em brushing their tracks out. I wish I had thought of it though, it sure would've saved us both a lot of puckerin'."

"That's the truth. I ain't sure there's enough leather left in the seat of my saddle to even sit down proper," Tig replied with a relieved smile.

As we turned into the ravine, the heat from the glaring noon sun intensified as it reflected off the solid rock walls that surrounded us. The sweltering air lay oppressively dormant, as the sand stirred up by the hooves of our horses hovered around us like a swarm of gnats before coming to rest on our sweat-soaked clothes.

The narrow trail, crossing between two large boulders, suddenly widened as it ducked underneath a large shadowy overhang. A welcoming breeze gently greeted us as we pulled our horses to a halt. We both sat in silent awe as the enormous canyons opened up below us.

The towering walls stood like silent monuments. Their pastel surfaces of pinks, blues, reds and greens softly blended together as though painted with the horizontal stroke of a wide brush. A small stream, which lay three hundred feet below us, slowly snaked its way down the middle of the valley floor. On either side of the stream, a stand of knee-high green grass silently swayed in the prevailing breeze.

"Of all the places we've been, I don't reckon I've ever seen anything quite so pretty as this," Tig said. "Have you?"

I was about to answer when suddenly I heard a loud thud. I felt my mare shudder beneath me as she let out an ear-piercing squeal. A split second later the crack of a gunshot reverberated off the canyon walls.

"Let's go!" I yelled as I sank my spurs deep into the ribs of my horse. With the fingers of my left hand laced into the thick black mane, I leaned low over Sadie's neck as we perilously sped down the treacherous trail. I felt my hand growing slick with her warm blood as gunshots continued slamming into the rock wall around us.

Nearing the canyon floor, I felt Sadie quickly beginning to falter. As she began stumbling, I quickly kicked my boots free of the stirrups. Suddenly her front end dropped from beneath me, launching me from the saddle as she went head-over-heels. I felt the air explode from my lungs as I slammed hard into the uneven ground. Sadie came to rest within a couple of feet from me, her legs flailing wildly as she thrashed about on her back.

Immediately jumping to my feet, I sprinted for a cluster of boulders fifty feet away. Bullets tore at the ground around me as I dove headlong into the cover. Lying on my back underneath the base of a large rock, I frantically gasped for air that seemed an eternity in coming. Within seconds, Tig came barreling into the small area, diving from his horse while on a dead run. Hitting the ground hard, he rolled against a boulder. His horse continued on a short distance before coming to a nervous stop.

Getting to his hands and knees, Tig scurried over to where I was. "Are ya' all right?" he asked excitedly.

Unable to speak, I nodded. As I lay still, my breath slowly began to return in short, erratic gasps. Several more gunshots ricocheted off the rocks before all fell silent.

Slowly sitting up with my back resting against a rock, I could hear the unnerving sound of my horse groaning in agony as she lay on her side. Her hooves were thrashing violently, tearing up the ground around her as she struggled for her life. Pulling my pistol, I cautiously peered around the rock. Taking careful aim, I felt a sickening in my stomach as I squeezed the trigger. The pistol bucked in my hand. Sadie's head immediately dropped to the ground, where she lay motionless. A thin trail of blood began to slowly trickle from the small round hole between her eyes.

Replacing the spent cartridge in my forty-five,

I looked at Tig. His eyes were wide as he nervously scoured the canyon walls. Trails of sweat streaked his dirt-covered face.

"Are ya' hit?" I asked.

He shook his head. "Naw, I don't think so," he said as he uncertainly gave himself a once-over before being thoroughly convinced. "They've got us in a hell of a predicament, Chance. What are we gonna do?"

Shaking my head, I said, "I don't know. But I know one thing, if we don't get that horse of yours it's gonna be a long walk out of here. Even worse than that," I added, "we've got to get to our rifles. Our pistols ain't gonna do much good in here."

Getting to our hands and knees, we crawled to the edge of the scattered boulders. Peering in between a gap in the rocks, we could see his horse standing thirty or forty yards away, his head down as he peacefully cropped mesquite grass. Contemplating my chances of making a run for the horse, a shot suddenly rang out. My heart dropped, as did Tig's horse.

I could see the air slowly deflate from Tig's body as he painfully stared at his fallen horse. A deep pain showed in his eyes before he lowered his head. "That was the only horse I've ever had," he mumbled. "My pa gave it to me the night it was born. That was the only thing my pa ever gave me."

When he raised his head again, I could see that the hurt had turned into a deep-rooted anger. "I'm gonna get 'em for this," he said through clinched teeth.

"I swear to God, if it's the last thing I ever do on this earth, I'm gonna kill ever last one of 'em."

As I sat watching Tig, I knew he had every intention of doing exactly what he said. One thing about Tig, he was as honest as the day is long. "We'll get 'em," I said. "But, in order for us to get them, we've got to make sure they don't get us first."

It seemed ironic to me that only minutes ago we had sat high upon the jagged canyon wall admiring the extraordinary beauty that stretched before us. Now sitting huddled next to these rocks, in a place known as Hell's Gate, with no rifles and both our horses dead, those same monumental walls threatened to be our eternal tombstones.

CHAPTER 5

Consumed with our own thoughts, we sat in silence as we hunkered down behind the safety of the cluster of boulders. Several times, I glimpsed the reflection of the sun off a gun barrel high on the canyon wall opposite of where we sat.

I could feel an anxiety creeping inside of me that I had never experienced before. I have known the bite of a bullet, as a scar that runs the length of my shoulder attests. I have seen a man's life end as I held a smoking gun in my hand. However, in those particular encounters, it had all happened very quickly. There had been no time to think, only react. All the thinking came afterwards. That is what it was ... it was *the time*. *The time* was what opened the door for the apprehensive feelings to rip and tear and grate at a man's nerves. *The time* was what made a man question, or wonder, or to even doubt. It was definitely *the time* that made our situation seem even worse, if that was possible. And right now, the minutes seemed like hours.

I have never wished for the cover of darkness as bad as I wished for it now. To make a move to retrieve our rifles before then I knew would be certain suicide.

With the sun starting its downward arc, I caught a reflection that somehow seemed different from the ones we had seen earlier. As I studied it closer, it dawned on me what it was.

"Dammit!" I said shaking my head.

"What? What's wrong?"

"Somebody came in behind us."

"How do ya' know?" Tig asked as he quickly turned and studied the trail that we had followed into the canyon.

"They're signaling them with a mirror."

Turning back, he looked high upon the far canyon wall, where once again the sun reflected from the mirror. I caught a glimpse of panic in Tig's eyes as he quickly pointed his pistol toward the mirror and hastily squeezed off a shot.

I realized that *the time* had been gnawing at Tig also.

"What are ya' doing?" I barked. "We don't have enough ammunition to waste on a shot like that!"

Tig lowered the pistol before he looked over at me. "I ain't ready to die, Chance," he said shaking his head. "Not here. Not in a place called Hell's Gate."

I saw a true fear in his eyes, a fear that I had never seen before. "Tig, listen to me," I said as I grabbed him by the shoulders. "Listen to me. We're not gonna' die, but we've got to stay calm. If we don't panic, we'll figure a way out of here. But we've got to stay calm."

I could feel his body begin to relax in my hands. "Are ya' okay now?" I asked as I relaxed my grip.

He slowly nodded. "Sorry, Chance. I don't know what came over me."

"That's okay," I said reassuringly. "I'll admit I'm scared too. I think somethin' would be wrong with us if we weren't a little scared. But I've got faith in us, both of us."

Tig gave a weak smile as we sat back and continued waiting for the sun to disappear.

The only opportunity we had of retrieving our rifles was when full darkness hit the valley floor. It was not a very good chance because I knew that whoever was out there would be waiting, knowing exactly what we would be planning. However, I could find no other options.

I felt my heart beating faster as the departing sun began casting its long, finger-like shadows into the depths of the canyon. Ever so slowly, the lengthening shadows inched closer to where Tig and I sat huddled in the protection of the boulders. Somewhere on the rim above us, a coyote cut loose with a high-pitched, lonesome howl. The notes bounced eerily through the otherwise silent canyons.

The pitch-black of night brought with it a cold crisp air that immediately settled onto the canyon floor.

"You stay here," I said as I peered into the darkness.

"I'm gonna go get my rifle."

"Ya' want me to go with ya'?"

"No. Just stay where you're at and cover me," I replied. "If they start shootin' return the fire, but make sure ya' move after ya' do. They'll be shootin' at the flame from your pistol just like you'll be doin'."

Tig nodded his head as I lowered myself to my belly. I felt a vulnerability sweep over me as I began to crawl from the security of the rocks. Other than a couple of spindly clumps of sagebrush, there was nothing to offer protection between my horse and me.

My breathing seemed unusually loud as I inched my way along on my stomach. Nearing Sadie's body, the stench of finality reached my senses as her bowels had emptied when death came. Reaching out, I placed my hand on her neck; it was cold and stiff. I could barely see my hand in front of my face as my fingers searched for my rifle. Feeling the hard butt of the Winchester, I slowly worked it back and forth before it loosened and came free of the scabbard.

Setting the rifle next to me, I hurriedly untied the leather saddle strings that secured my coat and saddlebags. The bag that was underneath my horse would not budge as I tried to pull it clear. After several attempts, I gave up and reached into the bag on top. Finding the leather pouch containing shells for my pistol and rifle, I hastily shoved it into my coat pocket. Reaching back into the bag my fingers closed around the small black diary. Before turning to crawl back toward the rocks, I grabbed my canteen. Out of the corner of my eye, I saw the spark of a match an instant before a flaming torch was hurled through the air. Scrambling to my feet, I sprinted toward the security of the boulders.

"There's one of 'em!" I heard a man shout an instant before gunshots poured into the glowing air around me.

I could see flames stabbing from Tig's pistol as I dove headlong at his feet. Jumping up, I fired several shots from my rifle at no particular target.

As I leaned against a boulder catching my breath, the glow of the torch began to fade to a flicker before it blinked one final time before burning out. "Could ya tell how many there were?"

"Not for sure," Tig replied. "Maybe four or five. I think there was maybe two behind us."

My mind was racing with thought, as I knew they held every advantage over us that was to be had. Not only were they above us, but they probably knew these canyons like the back of their hands, whereas we were stumbling around blind in this enormous maze. The only equalizer was the darkness.

"We've got to get out of here," I said as I looked to Tig. "They'll position themselves so that when the sun comes up tomorrow it'll be like shootin' fish in a barrel. And we'll be the fish."

"What about my rifle?" Tig asked. "And my coat?"

I could see Tig's teeth chattering as the cold night air had closed around us. "Here, take my coat," I said.

"Naw, I'm all right. Maybe later," he replied.

Remembering that the shallow stream ran from east to west, I said, "Let's follow the stream, it has to be going somewhere."

Knowing they would be waiting for us to make a dash towards Tig's horse, we silently slipped out from the boulders in the opposite direction. Under the cloak of darkness, we headed downstream.

Stumbling through the darkness for most of the night, we continued to follow the shallow stream as it meandered its way between the confines of the towering bluffs. Numerous times the sheer walls pinched so tightly together we had to walk in the stream itself, intensifying the extreme cold that racked our bodies. Though we traded off wearing my coat, it did little good as our pants were soaked to the knees and our boots squished with water at each step.

As the stars began to yield to a lightening sky, we depressingly found ourselves staring blankly at a sheer cliff that towered more than eight hundred feet above us. The small stream disappeared at our feet beneath the base of the box canyon.

A bleak mood gripped us both as we slumped to the ground next to the vanishing stream.

"Now what?" Tig mumbled through chattering teeth.

I merely shook my head, as I had no answer.

"Ya' know," he continued, "I don't even care much any more. I just want the sun to come up so we'll at least be warm when we get shot."

I found myself chuckling at the comment. "Yeah, I guess that does sound better than gettin' shot while we're freezin'."

Tig gave a nervous laugh as he glanced over at me.

As the first rays of sunshine reached the canyon floor, I sat staring at the base of the cliff where the stream disappeared. Suddenly I got to my feet and began shucking my clothes.

Tig, stretched out on his back in the sand next to me, quickly sat up. "What are ya' doing?" he asked with a puzzled look.

As I stood in my long underwear, I said, "I'm gonna find out where this water is going."

Tig hastily got to his feet. "You're gonna what?"

"I'm gonna find out where this water is going," I said as I stepped into the stream.

The water was no more than a foot deep where it vanished beneath the wall. Bending down I could see maybe six or eight inches of clearance above the water. The cavity that it flowed into looked to be barely wider than my shoulders. Kneeling down in the water, I stuck my head into the opening. The hole was pitch-black.

Water was dripping from my hair as I raised up and turned to Tig. "If I ain't back out in a minute or two, ya might want to try somethin' else."

"Are ya' kiddin me?" he stammered.

"You got a better Idea?" I asked.

He stood silent.

My heart was beating fast as I stared at the opening. Taking a series of deep breaths, I laid down in the water on my back, figuring I would have a better chance of breathing from this position. Putting my arms in front of me, I began squirming into the tight hole. Reaching up with my hands, I could feel the jagged surface of the low ceiling only inches above my face. My ears were below the level of the water, causing a low steady rumbling to reverberate inside my head. Pushing with my heels while pulling with my hands, I slowly inched farther into the dark cavity.

Having gone fifteen or twenty feet I felt myself beginning to panic as the dark narrow walls pinched tight on my shoulders. My breathing suddenly became short and erratic. I could hear my own words echoing in my ears as I began talking to myself. "You're okay. You're okay. You're okay."

Slowly my breath came back to me. I felt a long sigh of relief escape across my lips as I once again continued. Having gone what I estimated another fifty or sixty feet, I felt the ceiling suddenly begin to ascend to the point where my fingers could no longer reach it. Pushing myself into a sitting position, I reached up and still could not feel the ceiling. Cautiously standing up, my fingers only found emptiness above me. Blindly feeling around in the blackness, I found I was in what seemed to be a small room. Cautiously stepping from the shallow stream, I felt sand and small gravel beneath my bare feet.

With my hands out in front, my fingers traced the outline of the jagged wall as I slid my feet along on the dry surface. My toes bumped into what felt like a stick. Reaching down with my hands, I found a pile of dried branches that I figured had been swept into the passage during a previous storm at one time or the other. Taking a deep breath, I stepped back into the water and began traversing the same dark passageway.

As my head popped into the daylight, I could see Tig frantically pacing in circles. When he saw me, he came splashing into the water and yanked me up by my shoulders. "I thought ya' was dead!" he exclaimed. "Damn, I thought ya' was dead!"

"I'm okay," I said. "Let's go."

"Where does it go?" he asked anxiously.

"I don't know."

"Ya' don't know?"

"Nope. But I know there's a place in there we can at least hide. That's better than sittin' here and not having any chance at all."

Immediately he began unbuttoning his shirt.

"Just leave 'em on," I said. "It'll be easier than

carryin 'em."

I quickly pulled my clothes on over my drenched underwear. With our holsters draped over our shoulders and my rifle held in front of me, we quickly entered the stream and squeezed into the water-filled tunnel.

As we shimmied along in the cold water, a strange rumbling reached my ears. I smiled as I knew Tig was doing plenty of talking, the same as I had.

I stood up as I entered the small room. Reaching down I felt Tig's hands as he entered the room. Grabbing hold of his arms, I helped him to his feet.

"Step over here," I said as I guided him toward me.

"Dang, that was scary," he said as we both stood dripping water in the pitch-blackness.

"I've got some matches in my coat," I said. "But we need to get out of our wet clothes first so we don't drip any water on 'em."

Quickly stripping down to our bare skin, I felt around for some dried twigs and made a small pile in what I figured was the center of the open area. Finding my coat, I reached for the inside pocket and pulled out a small watertight bottle. Unscrewing the lid, I retrieved a match. Kneeling down, I struck the match on the rough surface of a small rock and touched it to the dried tender. Immediately it sprang to life as the flame hungrily lapped at the kindling. The room began to glow as I added a couple of larger sticks.

As we stood buck-naked around the growing

light of the fire, I looked over at Tig. "I sure hope for your sake you're just extremely cold," I said chuckling.

"What do ya' mean?" he asked before he questioningly looked down and caught my meaning. "I … I am cold," he stammered before turning his gaze on me. "Anyway, I don't see nothin' you've got that's gonna win you any free rides."

We began laughing, as we stood naked, soaking up the warmth from the blazing fire.

With the chill having left our bodies, we smoothed out a place in the sand and sat down. The cavern, now fully illuminated, was much larger than what I initially thought. The large circular room was approximately twenty-feet across, with the small stream flowing through the center. The concaved ceiling stood ten to twelve feet above the floor.

The jagged walls had several deep fissures showing the stress the mountain had been under over time. Tig quickly put them to use. Jabbing several sturdy sticks into the cracks he hung our wet clothes up to dry.

"What do ya' think about that?" he said, admiring his work as his white buttocks reflected the firelight.

"That'll work," I replied. I figured we would just get them soaked again when we exited through the stream, but I kept my thoughts to myself.

"Ya' know," he said, "we have about everything we need in here, except for one thing.."

I nodded my head as my stomach growled. "Yep, food."

"What I would give for a big juicy beefsteak right now," he said with a faraway look in his eye. "Maybe some taters, and biscuits or black-eyed peas and corn bread. Now that I think about it a dang ol' skinny jackrabbit sounds pretty good." Realizing the topic was only serving as a form of torture for us both, we let the conversation drop.

Reaching into my coat pocket, I retrieved my small black diary. Though the book and a short stubby pencil were wrapped tightly in an oilskin, the worn fringes of the pages were wet. Stacking several limbs next to the fire, I opened the book and sat it on top of them to allow the pages to begin drying.

"Ya' know, as long as I've known ya', I've always wondered what you was writin' in that book," Tig commented as he stared at the diary. "What's so important that needs to be written down?"

I shrugged my shoulders as I looked at the curled edges of the tattered book. "I don't know. I guess not really anything," I said. "It's not like I've ever done anything that was important, like Sam Houston and General Burleson fightin' the Mexicans or McKenzie whippin' the Comanche. I suppose, if nothin' else, it will at least let people know that I was alive."

I knew the answer I gave was vague and not definitive, but it was the only answer I could come up with. I didn't know why I so diligently kept my diary.

Maybe somewhere deep down I hoped that at least once in my lifetime I would do something or accomplish something that was worthy of being recorded. Maybe that was what my mother was hoping when she gave it to me six years ago. Tig seemed satisfied with the answer even though I was not.

As I continued to study the room I noticed what little smoke the dried wood produced was not only rising but was also exiting through a round jagged opening eight feet above the floor on the opposite wall from where I sat. Getting up, I walked over and looked up through the natural chimney. The opening was in solid rock, like the rest of the cavern, and about three feet in diameter. I could see no light but I did not know if I would be able to, as the shaft appeared to slant upward at a sharp angle.

Turning back toward the fire, I saw Tig tentatively stepping into the water that was departing from the cavern. I could tell that the exit was clearly larger than the entrance had been to the rock room, but not by much.

"You'd better be careful," I said as he lowered himself into a crouching position in the water and made his way toward the tunnel.

"I will be," he called over his shoulder as he crawled on his hands and knees before disappearing into the opening.

I came to realize the anxiety Tig must have felt earlier when I wriggled into the watery opening and left him standing there not knowing if I was dead or alive. I had a whole new understanding of the nerve-racking ordeal. Walking over to the opening, I bent down and worriedly peered into the dark opening.

After only a few minutes, I found myself calling to him in the water-filled tunnel. I got no response. Stepping back to the dry ground, I added a couple of sticks to the dying fire before nervously pacing around. Desperately searching for something to distract my anxiousness, I rearranged the drying clothes on the sticks that jutted from the cavern wall.

Though it seemed like an hour, it was probably only ten minutes before Tig came crawling back through the water and into the cavern with a wide grin on his face.

"The sun's shinin' out there," he blurted excitedly.

"Ya' made it all the way out?" I asked.

"Yeah, it's not bad. Once I got past the first twenty feet or so I cold actually stand up and walk the rest of the way out. I mean, I had to hunch over is all," he added.

Grabbing my long underwear, I took my pocketknife and cut a small piece of the material off at one of the ankles. Picking up my rifle and pistol, I sat down next to the fire and began carefully wiping them down as best I could.

Tig looked at me in confusion. "How come you're not puttin' your clothes on?" he asked as he began getting dressed. "Don't ya' want to get out of here?"

I did not answer at first as I continued cleaning my guns. Uneasiness pulled at me. Looking up, I said. "What if they're out there just waitin' on us? You know they figured out by now we came in here, don't ya' think they will know where we're gonna come out? They'll be watchin' both places."

I could see Tig thinking about it, but he dismissed the idea with a shake of his head. "I'm sure they figgered it out, but they wouldn't of had time to get out of that box canyon and make it all the way around the mountain."

He seemed very sure of his thinking, but I did not. The more I thought about it, part of it made sense. The longer we sat here the more time they would have of getting to the exiting stream, if they were not already there.

"Okay," I reluctantly agreed.

After Tig cleaned his gun, we put our damp clothes on and stepped into the water once again. I followed Tig as he led the way out.

CHAPTER 6

I felt the warmth of the westerly breeze blowing through the tunnel before I saw the sunlight of the outside. Tig, walking in front of me, excitedly hurried along as the opening suddenly came into view only a short distance ahead.

"Tig," I called out. "Wait."

I could tell his impatience was pulling strongly at him as he irritably stopped. "What?" he barked as he turned and glanced at me over his shoulder.

Looking past him into the beckoning sunshine, I said, "I have a bad feelin' they're out there waitin' for us."

"I swear," he complained bitterly. "You worry more than an old woman."

Turning away from me, he walked from the protective shadows of the cave into the openness of the blue sky. Once outside he raised his arms in triumph. "I told ya' there weren't nobody out here," he said as he turned and looked at me with a smile on his face.

"Come on Chance, let's get out of here."

I saw the glint of sun reflect off a rifle an instant before a gunshot thundered into the stillness.

"Tig!" I yelled.

I saw his body jerk violently as a bullet tore into his back. His face contorted with incomprehensive confusion as I ran toward him. As I desperately reached for him, he staggered into my outstretched arms.

A barrage of gunshots immediately poured into the entrance of the cave, ricocheting off the rock walls with screaming, high-pitched whines. I felt a tug at the sleeve of my coat as I hastily dragged Tig back toward the safety of the narrowing tunnel.

The searching bullets continued probing into the depths of the cave around us. I knew the only place that would be safe from the relentless hail of bullets was the rock room.

"You hang in there, Tig," I pleaded as I continued dragging him toward the cavern. "Don't you quit on me partner, I just got to get ya' back inside. Don't you quit on me."

He was moaning loudly from the pain each time I pulled on him. The water beneath us turned red with his blood.

The cave was dark as the small fire had burned down to a few glowing embers. Pulling Tig out of the stream and up on the dry bank, he let out a loud gasp before slipping into unconsciousness. I quickly added some kindling to the fire and coaxed it back to life. I continued adding sticks to the flame until the room glowed with a bright reflective light as I stripped Tig's shirt from him. Gently rolling him to his stomach, I felt my heart sink as I saw where the bullet had penetrated his back, high between the blades of his shoulders.

Tearing a small strip from his shirt, I gently began daubing at the blood from the seeping wound. My hands were shaking as I reached into my pocket and retrieved my knife. Tig unmercifully regained consciousness and began moaning as I held the knife over the lapping flame.

When he spoke, the words crossed his lips in a mere whisper. A pink, frothy foam dribbled from the corner of his mouth. "Chance? Chance are ya' here?"

"I'm right here, Tig," I said as I knelt beside the fire. The thin blade of the knife began glowing a dull red. "I'm right here with ya' partner, just like always. You just set still now and don't be movin'."

I moved from the fire and knelt next to him. His eyes were pinched shut, his face completely devoid of color.

"Tig, I gotta get this bullet out of ya'," I said, trying to hide the doubt in my voice. "You gotta lay still and not move."

"Is it ... is it bad?" he asked.

I sat silent for a moment, staring down at the trail of blood that dribbled from the bullet hole in his back. My throat clinched tight. "Yeah ... Yeah partner, it's bad."

"I … I thought so," he stammered. "It hurts like hell."

"I know it does, partner," I replied. "I know it does, but it's gonna get better. You're gonna have to hold still now, while I get this bullet out of ya'."

"Don't let me die here, Chance," he whispered. "Please, don't let me die."

My hands were trembling as I knelt over him. He let out a sharp cry as I began probing deep into his back with the sharp pointed blade of the knife. His body relaxed as he once again succumbed to the pain.

When I finally sat back, my hands were smeared red with his blood. "I'm sorry," I muttered. "I couldn't get it out. I'm sorry."

The hours slowly passed as I sat listening to his shallow, unsteady breathing. Exhaustion finally overcame me as I faded into a disturbed, restless sleep. Imprecise, fragmented images began filtering unorganized through my despondent thoughts.

"I'll be fine Mama," I said reassuringly. "Don't you worry about me none." Drops of water spilled from the brim of my hat as I turned and looked over my shoulder one last time. My mother, suddenly dressed in black, stood staring down at a grave, a dark veil covering her face. "I'll be fine Mama," I called but she did not look at me, she only stared at the freshly covered grave. I kept calling to her repeatedly, but she only stared down. Suddenly I was whisked along above the ground until I stood next to her. "I'm here Mama, I'm here." Her eyes never rose. As I

glanced down at the dark disturbed soil, my eyes slowly moved to the tombstone. CHANCE RYAN TUCKER. "No!" I screamed. "No! No! No!" The sun glared brightly in my eyes as it reflected from the surface of the shallow river. Upstream, Tig was calling me. "Chance, look!" He was holding a large gold nugget in his hand as he stood in the water, an exuberant smile on his face. "Look what I found." The large nugget glistened brilliantly in the sunshine. Suddenly a low thunderous rumble reached my ears. As I stood staring past Tig, a twenty-foot wall of water came tearing down the canyon behind him. Large pine trees were splintering like matchsticks as boulders the size of wagons tumbled and bounced like tiny marbles. I ran toward him calling his name. He turned to me, horror etched on his face. "Chance, help me!" he desperately pleaded. "Chance, please help me!"

I suddenly jerked awake to the sound of Tig's voice calling me. "Chance?" he beckoned with a whisper.

Sweat was pouring down my face as I panted for my breath. Moving next to him, I answered. "Tig, I'm here," I said. "I'm right here, partner."

"Chance, I need to tell ya' somethin' " he sputtered as he violently coughed a crimson trail of blood.

Carefully rolling him to his back, I balled my coat into a pillow and placed it beneath his head. Taking a strip of cloth, I daubed the blood from the corner of his mouth. "What is it?"

His eyes pinched tight as he gritted his teeth.

"Ya' know how I said my folks were poor and I left home so there would be one less mouth to feed."

"Yeah," I nodded.

"Well it ain't true," he said as he looked up at me. "Actually my folks have quite a bit of money. My father's a very successful merchant and my older brother is a lawyer. My younger sister married a banker in New Orleans and lives in a great big house on the delta." He paused as he slowly shook his head. "I never was as smart as the rest of 'em and I always felt my father was ashamed of me because of that."

"I'm sure that ain't true," I said.

He nodded his head before he continued. "It is. I didn't leave home because I wanted to, my father told me to leave and not come back 'til I made somethin' of myself. I really don't believe he thought he would ever see me again."

"Well, I don't know your father," I said, "and I hope ya' don't take this wrong. But if he believes that the only measure of a man is how much money he has, you're already more of a man than he will ever be."

A taut grin creased a corner of his mouth. "Thanks, Chance. I needed to hear that."

"Whenever we get out of here," he said before he paused, grimacing in pain, "can we go ahead and get that spread we're gonna buy?"

Reaching out I placed my hand over his. "You bet we can," I said as I felt a tear spill down my cheek. "That's gonna be the first thing we do when we get out of here."

"Good … good. That sure makes me feel better," he whispered as he closed his eyes. "I think I must be gonna get better, cause I don't really feel much of anything anymore."

As I sat holding his hand, his body shuddered one last time as he expelled a final breath.

My body wilted over his as though my heart had been torn from my chest. "I'll miss ya' partner," I said with a trembling voice as I clutched his hand. "I'll miss ya'."

As I sat holding Tig's lifeless body, I heard a low rumble toward the narrow opening from the box canyon. The shallow stream was soon reduced to a faint trickle. I realized they had rolled a boulder in front of the opening. One less opening they had to watch, I thought to myself.

Standing, I ran a sleeve across my face in an attempt to dry the tears from my eyes. Adding a couple of small sticks to the fire, I turned my attention to the round hole where the smoke escaped the rock room. Walking over to the opening, I stood staring at it for a moment before I jumped and grabbed the uneven rim. The surface was jagged, allowing my fingers to get a firm grip. Straining, I pulled myself into the constricted opening. Climbing my way higher into the shaft, I soon saw daylight.

"This is it," I said aloud. "This my way out."

Working my way back down, I dropped to the

cavern floor. Making a sling with a strip of material from Tig's shirt, I slung my rifle over my shoulder. Kneeling next to Tig's body, I crossed his hands on his chest before covering him with his coat.

"I'll see ya' Tig," I said as I laid his pistol at his side. "And the way it looks, I'll probably be seein' ya' sooner rather than later."

Grabbing the rim of the chimney, I quickly disappeared into the narrow shaft.

The natural chimney exited the mountain at a gradual angle thirty or forty feet above the floor of the valley. The rock hole was surrounded by several thick clumps of juniper. The branches from the stubby trees extending in front of the hole formed a thick barrier. Not only did the branches diffuse the small amount of smoke the dry-burning wood had created, but also kept the shaft hidden from view. Reaching out and separating the branches, I cautiously peered through the opening.

The top edge of the fiery-red sun was all that remained on the western horizon as dusk quickly set in. I sat, trying to get my bearings and the lay of the land. I figured the exit to the cave that Tig had walked out of was probably no more than four or five hundred feet from where I was and just around a gradual, slop-ing bend in the rugged mountain. Forming a mental picture of the location of rocks and trees, I waited. As the cover of darkness began taking hold, a gentle breeze carrying the smell of wood smoke came to me. Also riding the light wind was the distorted sound of men's voices.

The black of night finally arrived. The wait, while in reality was short, had seemed excruciatingly long as hatred and vengeance tore at me. Checking my rifle and pistol one last time, I crawled from the opening and carefully worked my way in the direction of the smoke.

I could see a glow from the fire against the dark sky before I could see the flame itself. I cautiously angled my way around the edge of the slope. Nearing the rock-strewn crest, I dropped to my stomach and crawled the final twenty feet. The fire below was extremely large, sending flames leaping high into the night. Silent shadows eerily danced against the jagged walls of the cave.

The immense fire was no more than a hundred feet from the base of the mountain, bathing the entrance of the cave in its unimpeded reddish-gold light. The shallow stream, trickling its way from the tunnel, reflected a glimmering of yellow as it quietly disappeared into the night. Below the fire were numerous large boulders.

As I lay watching, the dark silhouette of a man appeared in the midst of the rocks. Reaching through the protection of the boulders, he added more fuel to the fire as a shower of sparks leapt into the air. They had everything planned out. With the entrance of the cave brightly lit and the rocks affording them protection to keep the fire stoked, in their minds, all they had to do was wait for me and Tig to come out so they could slaughter us like a couple of sheep.

Dropping back below the ridge, I worked my way down through a sandy ravine before coming up behind where I figured the men to be. With the night being moonless, I nearly crawled into the midst of three tied horses before I heard or saw them. One of the horses immediately stamped a hoof and snorted. Instantly I dropped to my stomach and lay motionless.

"What got into the horses?" I heard a man ask.

The voice came from the far side of a stand of thick brush no more than forty feet from where I lay.

"Probably just some varmint," another man replied.

"Well, go check!" the first man said gruffly. "Hell, can't anybody do a damn thing around here without me havin' to tell 'em to!"

I heard a man mumbling under his breath as he came around the edge of the brush, walked over, and stood next to the horses. He was so close I heard him laboring with the buttons as he undid his pants to relieve himself. When finished he walked back around the brush. I followed close behind, stopping in the deep shadows of a cedar tree within easy spitting distance of the three men. The blaze from the large fire on the other side of the boulders reflected light off their faces. Not any of the men had I seen before.

"So, what was it?" a heavy-set, bearded man

asked.

The slender man who had walked out by the horses moments ago shrugged his shoulders. "I don't know."

"You don't know?" the bearded man exclaimed. "Did you even look?"

"I'm sure it was just some kind of varmint like I said it was," he uncomfortably replied. Walking over to the boulders, he looked toward the entrance of the cave. "So when's Bert supposed to be back from Clear Fork?"

I flinched when I heard the name mentioned. Surely, it could not be possible that the man they referred to was Bert Ross, the foreman of the Box-T. The thought kept going through my mind as I sat listening in the night.

The third man, who was leaning against the boulders sipping on a bottle of whiskey, scoffed, "He said he'd be back tonight. But he won't be. He won't be back 'til mornin', after he's done playin' with them saloon girls."

"Well, I ain't waitin' around forever just to kill these two-bit saddle tramps," the slender man grumbled. "They was stupid enough to stick their noses where it didn't belong. They might be stupid enough to stay in that cave 'til they starve. And that could take a long time."

"Ya'll, shut up!" the big man yelled. "Jim, if ya' don't want to be here no more go back to the ranch and tell Mister Ross ya' got tired of waitin' and see what he says."

I felt my blood begin to boil, as I now knew for sure that J.B. Ross, the man who had hired me and Tig, was the man who now wanted us dead.

"Well, I wasn't really gonna …"

"Keep your mouth shut then," the big man chided, cutting him off mid-sentence. "If either one of these fellas gets out of here alive they'll have a posse on us so quick there won't be a rock big enough to hide under. Not only that, Mister Ross and Bert will turn on us like rattlesnakes. Hell, they'll be the ones holding the end of the rope when they hang us."

"Hang us? How could that be?"

"I'll tell ya' how that could be," the big man snarled, growing more agitated. "They'll say we were the ones stealin' cattle all this time. Not only would that get them off free and clear, it would explain to the owners, come tallyin' time, how come the ranch is short four or five-hundred head of cattle. And the Ross's have the money and power to make it stick."

The third man began snickering before he took another swig off the bottle. "Damn, Jim," he said, wiping his mouth with the back of his hand. "You was callin' them two fellas in that cave stupid. If ya' ain't figgered all of this out yet you ain't none too bright yourself."

My mouth was dry, my heart pounding as I stepped from the shadows. "Keep your hands where I can see 'em," I said. I was surprised myself by the cold steadiness that sounded in my voice.

All three men slowly raised their hands as they turned toward me. Their faces were pale as though they were looking into the eyes of a ghost.

"Drop your pistols one at a time," I said as I held my rifle steady. "Nice and easy."

Slowly, each one emptied their holsters before again raising their hands in the air.

"Now, move over here together. I want ya' to be in a nice tight little bunch."

The slender man began to nervously talk. "Look mister, there must be some kind of mistake here."

"My name is Chance Tucker," I said calmly. "Which one of ya' killed my partner?"

They all stood silent, a look of contempt on their faces.

The slender man opened his mouth to talk as I squeezed the trigger. He screamed in pain as my bullet tore into his thigh. Dropping to the ground, he grabbed at his leg. He began whimpering as I pointed my rifle at him again.

"Which one of ya' killed my partner?" I asked again.

This time he quickly pointed at the big man. "It was him that done it!" he cried out. "It was Dave!"

"Shut up, Jim," the big man growled as he took a step backwards. "It wasn't my idea. It wasn't my idea at all. We was just doing what Mister Ross told us to do."

"I guess a fool can always find bigger fools to follow him," I said as I leveled my rifle at his belly. "You're gonna die real slow, just like my friend that you shot did."

"Hold on now, Mister. Please, I'm beggin' ya' please," he was pleading as my gun roared in my hand.

The impact of the bullet drove him backwards, slamming him into a boulder. Clutching his stomach, he cried out in pain as he slowly sank to the ground. He lay on his side moaning as blood began seeping from around his tightly clasped fingers.

The third man frantically took off running. I shot him twice in the back before he could reach the shadows.

The man I shot in the leg was desperately trying to crawl away, his wounded leg dragging behind him. His begging fell on deaf ears as I stood over him. As he covered his head, my rifle belched flame one final time.

Picking up their guns, I tossed them into the darkness. Walking past the roaring fire, I entered the mouth of the narrow cave.

After carrying Tig's body from the confines of the cavern, I placed him in the bottom of a steep ravine. Climbing back to the top of the gully, I stood silent in the obscurity of darkness before caving the sandy bank over top of him.

"It ain't over yet, partner," I stated flatly. "But it

will be soon. I promise ya'… it will be soon."

I quickly rummaged through the saddlebags that sat on two of the horses, taking anything that I thought would be of use to me. After stripping their saddles and bridles, I sent them thundering off into the night. Stepping into the saddle of a big bay gelding, I could hear the big man calling my name as he begged for the mercy of a suffering-ending bullet.

Turning the horse into the blackness, I rode away from the death-filled canyons.

As I listened to the steady drumming of hooves beneath me, hunger gnawed at my insides. It suddenly struck me that hunger was the only feeling I seemed to have.

Within minutes of Tig's death, all of the usual feelings seemed to have died inside of me. There would be no more laughter, or happiness, or even the simple enjoyment of watching a sunrise or sunset. There would now only be daylight and dark. Even grief and sadness had somehow already become a distant and unknowing stranger. In my heart, there were no longer any hopes or dreams or ambition to drive me, only a blind unwavering lust for vengeance and justice.

It was then I realized that I had entered Hell's Gate as one man and had come out another.

CHAPTER 7

The stripped bones of a jackrabbit lay strewn next to me as my small fire flickered and danced in the stiff westerly breeze. The meal, though scrawny, temporarily filled the emptiness inside my stomach. Lying back, I watched as scant delicate clouds silently drifted past a silvery crescent moon. Somewhere in the vast distance, a wolf called out to the night. The moaning howl carried past me before disappearing into the darkness like a thief in the night. After a short sleep, I kicked dirt over the ashes and stepped into the saddle heading west.

The sun was mere minutes above the eastern horizon when in the distance I saw a plume of white dust rising steadily into the air. Pulling my horse to a stop, I sat and watched. At first, I thought it might be mule deer or possibly antelope. However, I quickly dismissed the thought as the lumbering motion held truer to that of horses at a loping gait.

The towering dust quickly began to dissipate as the movement slowed before coming to a halt. The realization came too late to me as I saw a reflection of the sun off what appeared to be binoculars. The objects were three mounted horsemen.

Pulling my rifle from its scabbard, I pushed the bay into a gallop heading directly toward them.

Two of the men instantly headed north, their horses at a run. The third rider turned his horse and headed back west, the direction of Clear Fork, from which they had come.

I figured one of the riders to be Bert Ross, but at that distance I could not tell which one. I also knew with the lead they had on me there was no way I would be able to catch up to them, anyway. The one advantage that I briefly held, the element of surprise, was now gone.

"Now what?" I said aloud as I pulled my horse up and watched the disappearing trails of dust.

The three men back at Hell's Gate had undoubtedly called the cards right. However, instead of them wearing the tag of a rustler, it was I who would now be known not only a cattle thief but a killer as well. Within hours there would be a posse desperately searching for my trail, worked into a frenzy with the blatant lies of J.B and Bert Ross.

Some of the men who would be hunting me would be men of honor and integrity, men of the belief they were doing what was just and right. Unbeknownst to them, they would be riding alongside the true thieves and murderers. The thought of my own death did not disturb me. The thought of Tig's death going unavenged tore at my very soul.

I realized with the number of men hunting me there would be no way I could possibly get close to J.B. or Bert Ross. They would surround themselves with heavily armed men, while others continued scouring the surrounding country for my trail. I needed time to think ... to plan.

I had to find a place to lay low for a while. North or west was not an option, and east would take me back to Hell's Gate. Squeezing the bay horse into a trot, I headed south into the remote and desolate country.

As the rugged canyons disappeared behind me the land become relatively flat. Only spindly mesquite trees, cat claws and clumps of prickly pear broke the openness. The grass became sparse, as did water.

Riding through the empty, deprived land, my mind swirled around the events of the previous days much like the dust devils swirled in front of me as they twisted and danced across the barren terrain. At times, I felt myself being overwhelmed by the tragic storm that had suddenly engulfed my life.

The memory of Tig tore at my thoughts, unmerciful and unyielding. It seemed one minute we were laughing as he scraped cow manure from his boot, the next I was holding him in my arms as he painfully gasped his last breath. All for what? For the greed of a corrupt cattleman and his son? For the mere price of a few hundred head of cattle?

A deep-rooted hatred festered inside of me, the same as that of a rotting mesquite thorn. The hostility that drove me was intense and unrelenting. I knew, someday soon, that deep hatred would be responsible for the taking of my life, as well.

The dust, which trailed behind the hooves of my horse, settled on top of me as I came to a halt atop a small rise. Turning in the saddle, I checked my back trail. I saw nothing. The sight held no comfort for I knew it was only a matter of time.

To this point, I had ridden a straight trail south, more concerned with putting distance between myself and the pursuers than with the covering of my tracks. Now, as the ground became rockier, I grasped the opportunity to change that.

Dismounting, I reached into the saddlebags and retrieved a small burlap sack that had held a small amount of grain for my horse, but was now empty. Cutting the sack into four small pieces, I tied the sacking to the hooves of the horse. Leading the horse a short distance, I stopped and glanced back. There was not a single mark on the flat surfaces of the large rocks, no evidence at all of my passing.

The sacking would not last long, but it would cost the posse precious time as they would have to search for my tracks in the hot desert sun. Fixing my sights on a mesa that loomed so far off on the western horizon it appeared only as a small knoll, I swung into the saddle and turned the horse into the expanse of the arid wasteland.

As I rode west, a dry, hot wind began to intermittently blow. Throughout the day the winds continued to intensify, causing the sand to whip and batter me, stinging my face and eyes. The sand swirled and shifted as it poured over the rolls of the barren terrain, continually changing the landscape in front of me. On occasion, I would dribble some water from my canteen into my handkerchief and wipe my horse's eyes and nostrils clean. The big bay horse, with its head held low to the ground, continued to fight onward.

Nearing nightfall, I rode into a shallow depression and hunkered down with my back to the howling winds that drove the unrelenting sandstorm. The bay stood beside me as I clung to the leather reins.

When dawn broke the following morning, it was nearly undistinguishable from the night. The sun seemed helpless to penetrate the light-absorbing blanket of sand that continued to sweep across the desert floor. An unnatural darkness shrouded the landscape.

It was the morning of the following day before the winds exhaustedly ceased and the sky cleared. The sand slowly sifted back down to the playa as the fierce burning of the desert sun returned to reclaim its territory with a severe vengeance.

The deceptive powers of the desert proved to be unequaled as the mesa, which I thought to be a good two or three day's ride, turned into six. Reality hit hard as I stood staring at the mesa, which still loomed far off in the distance. For days, I had blindly stumbled in a wide circle.

My canteen had long rode empty. I dismounted and walked as my horse had grown weak beneath me. As the hours slowly melted together, I shuffled heavy-footed as the heat waves danced and shimmered around me. The bay's head hung low as it exhaustedly plodded along behind, its lathered coat layered with a fine chalkiness of the white alkali dust.

Water had proven to be as elusive as the mesa, always seeming to flee from my outstretched grasp. On numerous occasions, I found where water from a previous rain had pooled in the natural cup of a rock. But by the time I reached them the only remains were a cool dampness where the precious water had sat only the day before or possibly only hours before. The thirst of the desert heat continued to greedily lap the moisture in front of me.

The bright hovering sun seemed to sit stationary in the otherwise brassy sky, beating down relentlessly. Its brilliance reflected from the glimmering surface of the bleached desert sand, causing my eyes to burn unmercifully and a dull pain to throb steadily in my head. My tongue, swollen and dry, lay dormant on my cracked lips.

How long I walked before I realized the leather

reins had slipped from my fingers, I did not know, as the distorted reality that surrounded me had a way of hiding certainty. Unsteadily turning, I painfully strained to see through the intense glare. Several hundred feet behind me, the dark form of the bay horse lay on its side, its body seemingly suspended above the shimmering white sand.

I stood blankly staring, desperately trying to rationalize my scattered thoughts. But I soon gave up, as no rationale would come to me. Turning back toward the mesa, I continued on for reasons I no longer knew.

Many times, I found myself crawling before forcing my wavering legs beneath me only to take several unsteady steps and fall again. Finally, I lay unmoving, as there was no more strength to call on. There was no more will. There was no more desire. There was only the fiery hot sand of the desert burning against the side of my face.

CHAPTER 8

I was startled when I awoke. There was a damp coolness of a rag pressed to my forehead. Trying to sit up, I felt the touch of a hand on my shoulder and the sound of a soft reassuring voice. "Easy, *Senor*," a woman said. "You must lie still."

As I lay back, my body felt weak and unresponsive. My vision was somewhat blurred but began to slowly clear, as a dark form sat next to me gently touching the wet cloth to my face.

The young woman had a kind and gentle face, her complexion smooth and dark as were her eyes. Her silky black hair was pulled tight in a single braid that lay over a soft, delicate shoulder.

"I must've died and gone to heaven," I mumbled before closing my eyes against the dull pain that continued to throb in my head.

I must have dozed off, for when I again opened my eyes I was alone. A rectangle ray of outside light spilled into the small room from a window high upon a wall. The room was built of brown adobe bricks all neatly stacked and placed with great care by someone who evidently was very accomplished at the trade.

The corn husk-filled mattress rustled beneath me as I sat up on the edge of the bed and placed my bare feet on the dirt floor. It was then I realized that not only were my feet bare, but the rest of my body was bare as well. Quickly I pulled the thin blanket I had been lying underneath across my lap. A small kiva was molded into the opposite corner of the room from where I sat on the bed, a doorway draped with a serape on the other. A small table sat next to the bed, a clay pitcher containing water resting on top. A wooden-framed chair with a tightly stretched leather seat sat next to the small table. My boots sat on the floor next to the bed but my clothes were nowhere in sight.

Hearing a rustling on the other side of the doorway, I quickly pulled the blanket higher around my body.

When the young woman entered the room, she immediately cast her eyes to the floor and half turned around.

"I am sorry, *Senor*," she spoke uncomfortably. "But you should not be sitting up."

I felt a redness in my face as I drew the blanket tighter. With her eyes averted from me, she walked over and placed a bowl on top of the small table.

I could not help staring at her as she moved

across the floor with a subtle grace. The long white cotton dress she wore gently swayed with her movement. The fabric of the material was thin, highlighting the smooth roundness of her bosoms and drawn tight to her slender waist with a wide leather belt.

"My name is Chance," I said. "Chance Tucker."

She did not at first reply as she turned and headed back toward the doorway. Reaching the opening, she paused with her back to me. "I'm Rosario Cruz," she said softly before disappearing through the doorway. The serape momentarily swayed with her passing.

I sat staring at the doorway, before my attention was distracted as the aroma from the bowl reached my senses. Picking up the bowl of stew and a spoon that sat next to it, I hesitantly took a bite. The stew was hot and laden with fresh vegetables. The pieces of meat in the bowl I did not recognize, but the taste was very good.

After setting the empty bowl on the table I once again lay back on the bed. Sleep came to me quick and sound.

When I next awoke, it was to the sound of voices coming from the other room. One voice I recognized as Rosario's, the other was the voice of a man. How long I slept I did not know, but the window, which earlier had spilled sunlight, was now dark. The only light in the room came from the faint flickering of a candle that sat on the small table next to the bed. In

101

the dim light, I saw my clothes clean and neatly folded in the leather chair.

I continued to listen as I quickly began dressing. The conversation was in Spanish, of which I only had a vague understanding. Most words of the language that I was familiar with were rather useless in most conversations. The tone of Rosario's voice was meek and subdued, while the voice of the man was strong and held an agitated bite.

As I stamped my feet into my boots, I heard a wooden door slam hard against its frame. Standing up, I felt a light-headedness take hold of me as I teetered before gaining my balance. Through the opening of the window, I heard the crunching of gravel beneath footfalls before the steps slowly dissipated in the distance.

Reaching out with my hand, I moved the serape from the doorway. Rosario stood with her back to me, busily working over a cook stove. I cleared my throat as I stepped through the opening.

She quickly turned, a startled look on her face.

"I'm sorry, ma'am," I said. "I didn't mean to frighten ya'." Her features slowly relaxed as she stared at me.

"I was just gonna go outside," I said. "I figgered I could use a little fresh air, maybe it'll do me some good."

Taking a step toward the door, I felt myself swaying as I put my hands out and grabbed for the smooth surface of a table.

Rosario immediately ran to me, putting her arm around my waist. "You must sit down, *Senor* Tucker," she exclaimed as she lowered me into one of the four chairs that sat next to the table. Straightening up, she said, "You should not be up. But I suppose you are just like Diego, you probably think you always know what is best also."

There was a firmness to her words and a fire in her dark eyes I had not seen.

Not knowing exactly how to respond, I chuckled. "I suppose, I'm like most men in that way, ma'am," I said. "But I'm not sure if I'm like Diego or not. Is Diego your husband?"

She quickly turned back to the stove. "No. Diego is my brother," she scoffed. "But if all men are as controlling as him, I wish not to be married."

The tension was tight in the room. The softness in her voice, in which she had spoken earlier, had dissipated in the time I had been asleep. I laughed inside, as this was not the first time I had seen this happen. A different woman, a different place, but the same sudden change in demeanor.

"I should go outside," I again said as I cautiously stood up and headed toward the door. "Like I said earlier, maybe the fresh air will do me some good."

I could hear her mumbling in Spanish as I closed the door behind me. The night air was crisp and pure, bringing somewhat of a resurgence to my worn body. The stars shined brightly overhead as I moved away from the adobe dwelling that was built in the side of the cliff. Finding a large flat rock, I sat and listened to the sounds of the night. The hum of a darting bull-bat's wing reached my ears over the constant chirping of crickets. A dove softly called out but the call went unanswered. A lone coyote howled. Within minutes, a chorus joined in as the howling reached a crescendo before fading back into the security of the night.

Suddenly the sounds were replaced by a deafening silence. I heard the crunching of gravel underneath heavy footsteps before I saw the dark figure of a man emerge from the shadows. Standing up, I instinctively reached down for my pistol, but it was not there.

The man stopped a few feet away from me. The stars allowed only a silhouette, until a match was struck and touched to the end of a cigarette. The radiant light of the match reflected off the round, dark bearded face and the black eyes of a Mexican man.

When he spoke, his voice was flat and cold. "So, are you a murderer or a thief?"

I recognized the sound of the voice as the one I had heard earlier and realized the man standing in front of me was Rosario's brother, Diego.

He was a big man, matching my height of six feet, but he was much heavier than I was. His shoulders were broad and his barrel-shaped chest thick and powerful. The tone of his voice brought an ire to me, but before I answered, I put myself in his shoes and realized he had every right to be skeptical.

"Well, I guess it depends who ya' ask," I said. "Most men would say neither. But there are others who would say both."

"And what would the men who follow you say?"

"They're the ones who would say both," I said before pausing. "But they're the ones that are wrong."

I saw his face again as the end of the cigarette glowed a cherry red as he drew deeply. There was no expression on his chiseled features or in his deep voice as the smoke spilled over his lips and dissipated into the night. "You will leave here as soon as you are able," he said as he turned on his heels.

There were several questions I wanted to ask. *What had happened to the posse? Where were my guns? And how could I leave this desert on foot and hope to make it out alive?* However, he faded into the shadows before I had the opportunity.

Standing alone in the darkness, I felt a tiredness once again overtake my weakened body. Turning around, I sluggishly headed back to the adobe house in the cliff.

This time I knocked before entering. Rosario was sitting at the wooden table, a lighted candle flickering before her. The soft light reflected the silkiness of her long, coal-black hair. Her dark eyes seemed to hold a faint sparkle as she looked to me.

"Please sit down, *Senor* Tucker," she said as she stood up. "I'll pour you a cup of coffee."

I did not know if the coffee was what sounded good or if it was the opportunity to sit across the table from Rosario that was appealing. I decided it was irrelevant as I pulled out a chair and sat down. She placed a steaming cup in front of me before gracefully returning to her chair.

I took a drink of the coffee. It was hot and strong.

"I feel as though I owe you an apology," she said as her delicate fingers nervously fondled the cup in her hand. "I was sharp with you earlier," she continued, "for which I had no reason. At times Diego irritates me but I had no right to take my frustrations out on you."

"No apology is necessary, ma'am," I said. "There are times when things are a little stressful. I understand that as well as anybody."

"So, does that mean my apology is accepted or not?" she asked with a raised eyebrow.

"Yes, ma'am," I chuckled. "I suppose if it's that important to ya, I accept your apology."

"Fine then," she said as her thin lips parted in a smile. "Now, that was not so hard, was it *Senor* Tucker?"

"I reckon not," I replied.. "But since you asked somethin' of me, that means I get to ask somethin' of you."

"That sounds fair enough," she skeptically replied. "And what is it you ask of me, *Senor* Tucker?"

"I would appreciate it if ya' would just call me Chance. I take to that better."

"Very well then, Chance" she nodded. "And you may call me Rosa."

"Rosa is a very beautiful name," I said. "And it's most fitting for you." I saw her cheeks lightly blush in the dim light.

"Rosa, I have a few questions I sure would like to ask ya."

She smiled. "I have many questions for you as well, but tonight is not the time. Maybe tomorrow when you are more rested."

With my cup setting empty, I stood up and pushed the chair beneath the table. "If ya' would tell me where my bedroll is or which blanket to use I'll make my bed outside. I don't want to be a burden on you and Diego."

"Tonight you sleep in the bed," she replied. "You have been through much and much rest is needed."

I knew there was no reason to argue the point. In the short time I had talked to Rosa, I had the feeling it would be a wasted effort.

"Okay," I nodded. "But only tonight."

After undressing, I laid back on the soft bed. I found my thoughts consumed with the beautiful Mexican girl. There was something special about her. It was not only her rare beauty, which I found provocative and exciting, but something else, something mysterious and elusive. What was such an attractive woman doing in such a place as this? A woman with such beauty that could afford her a pampered life in any city with any man of her choosing. Yet, she was here on this lonely mesa in the grips of a harsh desert. I thought myself foolish for thinking of such things. What difference did it make? My life was destined. I could not change my past and I could not change my future. There could not be a wife and a family such as most men desire in their lives. There could only be vengeance and a harsh justice for the murder of my best friend. The only thing my future guaranteed was there would be more killing before I myself would be killed. A despairing sleep soon overcame me.

CHAPTER 9

I was up and dressed as the pre-dawn light first appeared in the small window. The main room was empty as I walked through and stepped outside. This was the first time I had seen outside the adobe dwelling in the daylight and I stood speechless at the sight that greeted me. Somehow, amidst this harsh and forbidding desert, a Garden of Eden sprawled before me. A valley of more than a thousand acres lay shrouded in a veil of early-morning fog. The tops of trees protruded from the smooth layer of fog like buoys lost on a calm sea. As the first gleams of sunlight began to shower over the sheer rock walls that encircled the valley, a thousand tiny rainbows sparkled and danced in the fine mist.

From where I stood, there was a thin trail that wound its way down the side of the cliff and disappeared into the haziness below. Sitting down on a rock, I watched as the sun gradually crept higher into a clear empty sky. The misty fog began to slowly waver before dissipating as the preeminent desert sun once again took hold of its domain.

I was lost in my thoughts from the night before when I heard Rosario's voice. "It is beautiful, is it not?"

I quickly turned and she was standing no more than ten feet behind me. "I must be gettin' lax," I said as I stood up. "I never heard you walk up."

She smiled. "That is okay. You are safe here."

The words somehow had a calming sound to them. I had not felt safe since entering the precarious trail into the canyons known as Hell's Gate. The place where my life abruptly changed when my best friend, a man I loved as a brother, died in my arms.

"My brother, Diego, wishes to speak to you," she said as a solemn look came over her face. "I must tell you he is a hard man. He is a man that carries much trouble in his heart. Some of the trouble I feel is justified ... some I feel is not. But either way he carries it with him always."

I understood the words she used to describe her brother, as it would be the same words I would use to describe myself. The reason for his torment I did not know, the reason for mine I knew all too well.

I nodded as I looked into her dark eyes. "I'll go see Diego," I said. "And whatever he decides I'll go along with. But, I want you to know one thing, I appreciate ya' both for what ya'll have done for me."

I saw tears forming in her eyes before she

quickly lowered her head. I wanted to reach out and pull her to me to somehow try to console the loneliness I saw in her, but I knew I should not, for to do so would only add to the emptiness that already seemed to surround her. My time here was but a resting place, for the task at hand was more important than Rosa, or me, or anyone else.

"Where is he?"

She pointed to a path that faded off to the east, but she never raised her eyes to look at me.

The pathway was steep and winding as it weaved in between large boulders that hugged the walls of the cliff. The crunching of sand and gravel beneath my boots seemed loud in the otherwise stillness of the serene valley. The fog had lifted and an expanse of greenness, seeming so out of place, opened around me.

As I walked around a sharp bend in the path, I saw Diego standing before me; his face was dark and unfeeling. I stood silent, waiting for him to speak. It was long in coming. I felt his searching eyes measuring me, trying to understand what he did not know.

When he finally spoke, his words were blunt and to the point. "I think it is time for you to go."

I nodded as our eyes held steady. "I understand," I said. "But before I go, I want ya' to know the truth. Not only the truth of how I came to be out in the middle of the desert but the truth of what I have to do."

He did not respond but his eyes did.

"What I have to do is not something I would've ever wished for," I said. "It's something that I know will destroy me when it's done. But it's somethin' I have no control over. It has somehow become my fate … a fate I can't deny."

As I told him of the story of the Box-T and the canyons of Hell's Gate and the death of Tig Jones, he listened expressionless. When I finished I sat down as the words of my own story, untold to anyone, weighed heavy on my heart. He stood before me, silent and stoic, like a large serrated piece of granite. As I watched, his body slowly relaxed as the look on his face seemed to soften if only a bit. Sitting down across from me, his dark eyes slowly scanned the majestic canyon around us.

"I understand the feeling," he said as his jaws clinched tight. "Sometimes men as ourselves are left with no say in our own lives. There are things that drive us that most could not or will not ever understand. Many times these things that drive us are beyond our control. It becomes life itself."

What it was that controlled his life, he did not say and I did not ask. I figured if it was something that he had wanted me to know he would tell me.

As we sat silent the only sound was the wind, the only movement was the swaying of the trees and the bending of the grass. A shadow danced over us as a red-tailed hawk, with wings spread wide, rode the warm updrafts toward the blazing sun.

Glancing over at me, he said, "The men you spoke of no longer pursue you." I immediately looked up as the words surprised me. "I found their tracks where they turned around. They were probably five or six miles behind where I found you."

"How did you find me?"

"I was watching the dust from the top of the mesa," he said as he nodded his head up toward the top of the cliffs. "I was watching the buzzards as well. I have to admit they were disappointed at my arrival."

I grinned at his words. His expression did not change but there was a hint of humor in his dark eyes. He stood up and took a couple steps down the path before he stopped and turned around. "Maybe you should stay a little longer," he said. "A man should have a plan before he rides to his death."

With that, he left.

I sat a while longer, thinking on what he said. His words were disturbing. Like most men, I had spent my entire life planning on how to live. It had never occurred to me that now I must plan how I was to die. The more I thought about it, the more ominous those thoughts became.

The sun was waning in the desert sky by the time I headed back toward the cliff dwelling. Long before the adobe came into view, the smell of tortillas cooking reached my nose. As I rounded the last bend in the trail, I saw my saddle as well as the rest of the tack from the bay horse setting next to the door. My rifle and pistol sat atop the saddle.

Also setting alongside the other items was a washbasin, a sliver of soap and a razor. I smiled at Rosa's not-so-subtle hint as I ran my hand along the rough stubble on my chin.

Standing in front of a small mirror that was tacked to a tree, I lathered my face with the soap. Taking the razor in my hand, I looked into the mirror. At first, I was taken aback at the reflection that stared back at me. The face seemed extremely gaunt; the green eyes sank deeply into the desert-burned face. It was a face that I hardly recognized.

I had just finished shaving and dumped the water from the basin as Diego came walking up the trail. His clothes were covered in a fine dust, as they had been on each previous occasion that I had seen him. His eyes were showing a deep fatigue as his broad shoulders drooped with weariness. He nodded as he filled the basin from the water barrel that sat next to the dwelling. As he washed, my curiosity tugged hard at me.

What could he possibly be doing in this remote canyon that would leave him covered in dust to such an extent every day? And what kind of work would leave a man as strong and powerful as Diego worn to the bone?

One thing I did know, Diego was a man of few words and in all likelihood I would never know the answers to my questions.

The sun disappeared behind the canyon walls as I followed Diego into the adobe house. Rosa turned and smiled at me as we sat down at the table. Her eyes lingered as I ran my hand over my smooth chin. I heard her softly giggle as she turned back around and continued preparing the meal. Diego's eyes glanced between the two of us but he said nothing.

My mouth was watering as Rosa began placing food on the table. I waited as Diego filled his plate with black beans and some type of shredded meat. As he opened a clay bowl, steam rose from the fresh tortillas. Rosa patiently waited as she motioned to me. After filling my plate I waited for her, Diego did not. His plate was nearly half-empty before we took a bite. The meal was eaten in silence. I figured that was probably one of Diego's habits that did not set well with Rosa, the same as it would not set well with most women I had ever known.

Soon as Diego wiped the juice from his plate with the last bite of his tortilla, he immediately got up and went outside.

"This sure is good," I said as I looked over at Rosa. "You're an excellent cook. Is there anything you're not good at?"

She paused long before she finally replied. "Being alone so much," she said as she delicately picked at the food on her plate. "But, it is a life I have come to accept."

After we finished eating, I helped Rosa clear the

table. As she put a pot of coffee on to boil, she said, "Tell me about your friend, Tig."

I smiled, as I sat thinking back of all of the memories. "You would've liked him," I said. "He was quick to laugh, and had a smile that would light up a dark room. He had a heart as big as the horse he rode and would do anything to help out a friend, or even a stranger, in need. He was the kind of man that would pick up a mesquite switch and fight a grizzly bear if that's what he thought needed to be done." I paused as I chuckled at the memory of Tascosa and Jack Morgan. "That didn't always work out very well … for either of us. But I guess the thing that was more important than anything else … he was my best friend."

Rosa smiled as she reached over and placed her hand on top of mine. "You are right. I believe I would have liked him also."

We sat and talked well into the night. The conversation was pleasant and I caught myself laughing numerous times. At first the sound of my own laughter seemed strange, for it was an emotion in me that I believed had been buried alongside of Tig. In some peculiar way, it disturbed me. I felt as though by allowing myself enjoyment, I was somehow turning my back on my best friend. I knew the thought was foolish and far from the truth. Even knowing such thoughts were irrational, I still felt them and the feeling left me uncomfortable.

As the candle burned down to a flicker, I

hesitantly stood up. "I reckon I need to go get my bed-roll and find a place to bed down for the night," I said. "Thank you again for the fine meal and the excellent company."

She smiled as she followed me to the door.

As I stepped through the doorway, she called to me. When I turned her soft hands reached for mine. I felt my pulse quicken as we looked into each other's eyes. I wanted to pull her to me and feel her warm body next to mine. I wanted to taste the softness of her lips. I could see the same desire in her beautiful dark eyes and I could feel the passion and yearning in the touch of her warm, delicate hands.

"Good night," I said with reservation as I turned and grabbed my bedroll and made my way into the darkness. After walking down the trail a ways, I stopped and looked back. Rosa was still standing in the doorway, her slender body outlined by the candle that softly danced behind her. I wanted to run back to her and take her into my arms and tell her of my strong feelings for her, but I knew I could not. To do so would only add to her loneliness. And I now realized it would add to the deep emptiness inside of me as well. I knew I had to fight the feelings I was having, because with me there was no future. There could never be a future. There could only be an ending.

Walking down the trail that I had taken earlier in the day when I went to meet Diego, I found a relatively flat area covered in a soft mat of thick grass. Rolling out my blankets, I stretched out as a large yellow moon began rising above the serrated rim of the canyon. The bright moonlight, filtered by the full branches of a mesquite tree that stretched above, dappled the ground around me.

I was nearly asleep when a strange sound reached my ears. I sat up and listened as the distant noise came again. It was a sound I could not place at first, but I immediately recognized it as not being a normal sound of the night.

Getting to my feet, I strapped my gun belt around my waist. The heavy feel of the forty-five resting on my hip felt reassuring. Quietly picking my way down an obscure overgrown trail, I followed the muffled sound that had awakened me. Numerous times, I paused to listen before continuing into the darkness. Cautiously working my way through a mott of mesquites, I glimpsed a faint reflection of light upon the canyon wall. The light, dim and indistinct, seemed to be spilling from the depths of a cliff, well above the valley floor.

Loosening my pistol in its holster, I carefully searched for a pathway that led up the sheer cliff that stood above me. The path, when I found it, was nearly undetectable. I could tell that great lengths had been taken to keep the trail hidden. The sound, when it again reached my ears, struck a chord of familiarity.

Having spent time in numerous gold and silver boom towns, I suddenly recognized the sound as the scratching of the earth deep within the bowels of the mountain. As I followed the narrow trail upward, the glowing light in the mine grew more distinct, as did the metallic sound of a pick or sledge repeatedly striking a hardened surface with a steady, methodical rhythm.

I pulled my pistol as I crouched low and stepped into the opening of the shaft. The floor was littered with rocks of all sizes; some mere pebbles others weighing five hundred pounds or more. A scant pathway led between the rubble. Cautiously following the path, the sound of the pick grew louder as I crept farther into the shaft. Peering around a boulder half the size of a horse, I saw Diego, illuminated by the glow of a coal-oil lantern, swinging a double jack in an attempt to bust a large boulder. He was bare-chested, his muscles rippling with each swing of the heavy tool, his labored breathing coinciding with each powerful swing.

After watching a few minutes, I eased my way back out of the tunnel. As I left the entrance, I stopped and picked up a rock the size of my hand. After walking down the trail a ways, I reached a clearing in the brush. Holding the small rock up toward the moonlight, I slowly turned it in my hand, looking for any type of reflection or sparkle; I could not see any trace of minerals. Maybe in the daylight it would look different. There had to be something there, why else would Diego be putting forth such effort? And from the look of the shaft, he had been putting in that type of effort for an extremely long period of time. Lying back on my bedroll, I fell asleep, the rock setting next to me.

The rising sun brought a sparkle to the dew that coated the thin blades of the buffalo grass around me, but to the rock, it did not. After turning the rock repeatedly in my searching hands, I shrugged my shoulders and pitched it out into the brush. It just seemed another unresolved question in this valley brimming with intrigue and mystery.

CHAPTER 10

I felt my body growing stronger with each passing day, as did my growing desire for Rosario Cruz. The desire was a feeling that I did not welcome, but it seemed beyond my power to overcome.

In an effort to combat my yearnings, I spent much of my time exploring this beautiful valley that lay hidden like an emerald in the otherwise bleak desert. A spring bubbling from the base of the canyon floor flowed the length of the valley, its water running pure and clear. With this moisture, the gramma and buffalo grass grew tall and green, stout of stem and rich in nutrients. I found where the stream had been diverted and dammed in numerous places, forming deep pools that not only flood-irrigated a significant vegetable garden, but also spread life-giving water to the abundant amount of trees that flourished in the secluded valley. A large assortment of vegetables and even fruit trees appeared to thrive in the rich, fertile soil.

There were eight to ten head of goats grazing the tall grass, some bred for meat, several for milk. On sporadic occasions I glimpsed mule deer, which would have had to be hunted sparingly in order to sustain their population in such a confined area. According to their appropriate population, they had been harvested in such a predetermined manner. Also free to roam the valley were twenty head of horses. Confident of my knowledge of horses, I determined the small hardy animals to be of Spanish descent, possibly Spanish Barbs that had been brought to this country during early exploration by the Spanish Conquistadors hundreds of years prior.

As I continued my exploration, I found four distinct and well-used trails. The trails began steeply at the floor of the valley and wove their way upward before breaking out atop the peaks of the encompassing cliffs. With the use of the pathways, a man afoot had a view, not only of the entire valley, but an unabated view of the surrounding desert in all directions as far as a man could see.

As I sat atop the mesa, I understood how Diego had not only found me in the desert, but was able to see the pursuit of the posse miles behind me.

One morning after a hasty breakfast, I followed Diego from the adobe into the predawn light. He stopped as he heard my footfalls behind him.

"Ya' know," I said as he turned and inquisitively looked at me, "I would be glad to help ya'." He stood silent, his dark eyes questioning. "I don't know for sure what you're looking for, but I do know two men working together can get there twice as fast. Wherever *there* is," I added.

I could see him contemplating the idea before he finally nodded his head. "Follow me," he said as he turned and led off down the trail.

He moved with the ease of a man much smaller than his large frame, a man who was used to walking and climbing most everywhere he went. He did not move like most men that I knew, men who were accustomed to being horseback and only walked when necessity dictated, and then bitterly complaining each step of the way.

Entering the cave, we walked through the rubble of busted rocks before we reached the back wall. The cave was only slightly higher than our six-foot heights and half again as wide. I was surprised to see that the back wall was not solid, as I had supposed it would be, but was actually huge boulders all separate but tightly packed together. As I looked more closely at the walls of the tunnel in the daylight, I could tell it was not a man-made tunnel at all, but a cave.

Without saying a word, Diego handed me a sledgehammer and then picked up one of his own. Setting his feet shoulder width, he swung the heavy tool, striking a boulder with a solid thud. Widening my stance, I did the same. Within minutes, we were pounding the rock, alternating swings as a ringing cadence filled the tunnel. When the big rock ultimately crumbled from the barrage of smashing blows, together we rolled it out of the way and attacked the next one with the same persistence.

The coal-oil lantern had long been lighted before Diego set his sledge down. "That is good for one day," he said as he approvingly nodded.

Setting my hammer aside, I reached for my shirt. My upper body was shining with sweat and covered with a fine layer of white dust. I felt my muscles aching and threatening to knot with cramps as I struggled to button my shirt. Diego smiled as he grabbed his shirt.

As I followed Diego from the cave into the night, I said, "I suppose one of these days you're gonna' tell me what we're doing?"

"One of theses days," he said as he turned down the trail that led to the adobe. "One day soon."

After a meal that was eaten in relative silence, due to the fact I was so exhausted it was all I could to chew my food, I slipped through the doorway and headed down the path to my bedroll. Walking through the trees another fifty feet, to a place where the stream had been dammed to form a pool, I removed my clothes and lowered myself into the shallow water.

Sitting on the rocked bottom of the small pond, the cool refreshing water came to just below my neck. I leaned my head back on the soft grass that covered the bank. I dozed off. When I woke, I was shivering, as the desert night was brisk even though the days were hot.

Stepping from the cool water, I dried myself off with my shirt before crawling into my bedroll.

The following week the routine was much the same. The only difference was I could feel my body growing stronger each day and the pained muscles and extreme fatigue grew less. The time spent with Rosa was mostly during meals. I noticed she had become extremely quiet and subdued, and even though she still greeted me with a smile on each occasion, it was short and fleeting. I could see the loneliness in her eyes again, the loneliness that had begun to fade during our previous time together. I felt bad for her and I felt bad for myself as well, but I knew it was the way it had to be between us. It could never be anything else.

Diego continued to work like a man possessed. He did not share the reason with me until one day as darkness set in and the glow of the lantern reflected from our sweaty, dirt-covered bodies.

Setting the double jack down, he took a seat on a large rock. He sat in silence for several minutes, his dark eyes staring forlornly at the back wall of the tunnel. The rock had all been removed, leaving only the smooth, natural, back wall of the cave. "This is not the first cave such as this that I have cleared," he said. "It is only one of many."

Sensing our day was done and Diego was for the first time interested in talking, I put my double jack aside and sat down.

"This mesa has probably fifty such caves as

this," he said, still staring ahead. "Some deeper, some shallower, but all that have to be searched. It is a curse I have. It is the same curse that my father had. It is a curse so strong that it drove my mother to abandon us when I was only a little boy and Rosa even younger. But even with the leaving of my mother, a woman my father had great love for, he never wavered in his search. Never once did he doubt that one day he would conquer this canyon and uncover the possessions that it held hidden for hundreds of years.

"He should have doubted, for in the end this mesa beat him and broke him down until he was a frail old man before his time. Still he worked until one day a tunnel caved in and claimed him forever. In a way, I guess the mesa respected him and mercifully put him out of his misery."

I still didn't understand what it was that his father had searched for his entire life. Nor what it was that drove Diego to be following in the same footprints, the footprints that led his father to an early demise. What was it in these boulder-filled caves in this forgotten mesa in the middle of the desert that was so powerful and controlling that grown men had no choice but to search? What is so intoxicating to a man's senses that he willingly surrenders to the compulsion even if it means sacrificing life itself? I nodded my head as the answer came to me. It had to be a woman or gold. One thing I did know was there sure wasn't any woman that would be worth much after being dug up. Gold, on the other hand, is a very different story.

"Tomorrow I go for supplies," he said, "maybe you should come with me."

I wasn't sure if Diego was asking me to go because he needed help, or if he just cottoned to my company, or if he didn't want me to be here alone with his sister. I figured without much effort that he didn't want me to be alone with Rosario. That was probably a good idea. With a woman as beautiful as Rosa around a man begins to weaken over time, just as I was.

"All right," I nodded. "I've been wantin' to ride one of those mustangs ya' have anyway."

Diego stood up to leave. "In the morning we go then," he said. The expression on his face was as close to a smile as I had seen from Diego as he disappeared into the night.

It seemed I had no more than went to sleep when I was awakened to find Diego leading four horses down the trail in the dark.

"Are you ready, amigo?" he called.

"Yeah, I was up," I lied, as I wiped the sleep from my eyes and hastily began getting dressed. Staring up at the stars as I tucked in my shirt, I said, "It don't look like it's much past three o'clock. What time is it, anyway?"

"It is two-thirty," he replied.

"Two-thirty!" I quipped as I stamped my feet into my boots. "I thought cowboy'n started early."

"It is a long, hot trip," he said. "It is better to

start while it is still cool."

I was surprised to find Rosa with coffee boiling and breakfast prepared as we led the horses to the adobe.

After saddling our horses by the glow of a coal-oil lantern and placing empty packsaddles on the two extra horses, we quickly ate breakfast. Rosa seemed withdrawn as she watched us step into the saddles. Without saying a word, Diego led off down the trail.

Standing up in my stirrups, I adjusted the saddle underneath me. I felt Rosa's hand touch my leg. "You be careful, Chance Tucker."

"I'll do that," I replied, smiling down at her. "Is there anything I can bring ya' back from town?"

She nodded as the soft moonlight reflected from her silky hair. "Yes," she said, "Yes there is … you."

Smiling, I reached down and put my hand over hers. "I have every intention of doing just that."

Grabbing the lead rope to a packhorse, I squeezed my heels against the ribs of the mustang. I felt the horse hump its back underneath me before he spiritedly stepped out. "I'll see ya' soon," I called over my shoulder as I hurried to catch up with Diego.

The trail was an obscure one. I doubted even in daylight if I would have been able to find it. Following the narrow, twisting trail, it took a while before we exited the clandestine valley through a mere crack in the sheer exterior wall of the mesa. The desert lay before us, the white sand glowing fluorescent in the pale, bluish light of the moon. Saguaro cactus stood like an army of soldiers, their up-stretched arms casting a shadowy figure on the desert floor.

Riding alongside Diego at a trot, the sand quickly passed beneath the hooves of the Spanish mustangs. Nearing noon, with the sun high above us, Diego turned his horse into a shallow ravine. The sound of dripping water reached my ears as we pulled our horses to a stop and dismounted. At the head of the small ravine water trickled down the face of a cluster of rocks, forming a small pool beneath them.

Sitting in the shade of the gully, we ate tortillas as the horses drank their fill of the cool water.

"Many years ago," Diego said as he watched the horses, "there was a story told to my father of a Spanish explorer, Jose De La Vasquez, who had found much gold in a mountain range west of here known as the Superstitions. Leaving the Superstitions for Santa Fe, with the heavy gold loaded on many burros, he and his men were followed by a band of Mescalero Apache. The army of Spanish soldiers with Vasquez was a small one compared to the large band of Indians. Desperately seeking refuge, they found the hidden opening that led into the lost valley. Knowing it was only a matter of time until the Apache would force their way in, Vasquez and his men hastily hid the gold in one of the caves inside the mesa. Knowing that their chances of surviving were not good, they placed black powder in the mouth of all of the caves they had found. Soon as the Apache fought their way into the valley, Vasquez signaled his men to set off the charges. The entire mesa trembled and shuddered. After a brief, but bloody battle, Jose De La Vasquez and all of his men were slaughtered. The knowledge of which cave held the gold died with them."

I wrinkled my brow as I thought about his story. Stories of hidden treasures and lost gold mines were a common conversation anywhere men gathered. I had never put much stock in such tales, but there was little doubt that Diego, as well as his, father believed it unwaveringly.

I took off my hat and wiped the sweat from my brow as the sun found its way into the disappearing shade. "I've heard a lot of stories similar to this one. What makes ya' think this one is true? Have ya' ever found any gold in there?"

I could see a look of irritation on Diego's face at my questioning. He shook his head. "No, not the gold of which I seek." Reaching into his pocket, he tossed me a silver coin. "Me and my father both found a few coins such as this one."

I slowly turned the irregular-shaped coin in my hand. The coin was about half the size of a U.S. silver dollar but it was well worn and the striking hard to identify. I was finally able to make out what appeared to be a cross centered with lions and possibly castles in each quadrant on one side of the coin. On the other side, the marks were indistinguishable.

"So how old ya' reckon this coin is?" I asked as I handed it back to him.

"No one can tell me for sure," he said as he returned the coin to his pocket. "But one man told me he figured it to be close to three hundred years old."

"So, ya' found these coins in one of the caves?"

"No," he said. "The coins were found on the valley floor. That is where I figured the Spanish soldiers fell from the arrows and lances of the Apache."

Maybe there was something to Diego's story. If the Spanish coins were found in the valley, it would make sense that the Spaniards were at least there at one time or another. I have seen men chase pipe dreams with much less evidence to go on than the silver coin that rode in Diego's pocket.

CHAPTER 11

Darkness had long settled over the small desert town of San Ramon as we pulled our horses to a halt on the outskirts of the sleepy village. Other than the barking of a dog and the faint strumming of a guitar, the town lay tranquil in the desert night.

Sitting our horses, Diego's dark eyes carefully scanned the small town and its surroundings. "This is not a very nice place," he said. "I think it is best if you stay here. The Mexican people here don't even like Mexicans from other places, much less gringos."

"If it's such a bad place, why do you come here?" I asked as I leaned my arms across the horn of my saddle. "Is this the only place within a day or so ride of the mesa?"

He shook his head. "No, there are three such villages as this. I go to a different one each time I need supplies." After pausing, he added, "No matter where I go there are people that try to follow me back to where the gold is hidden."

I paused as I thought *what gold?* For fifty years, according to what Diego said, he and his father had searched for the supposedly hidden treasure. I believed him when he said they had never found any such cache of gold.

"That's all right," I said as I looked over. "It ain't the first time I've ever been followed. And anyway, I don't like most Mexicans much either."

That was the first time I ever saw a smile cross Diego's face. It quickly disappeared as he put his horse into a walk.

The hooves of our horses kicked up dust at their feet as we turned down the narrow street. Most buildings sat dark other than the dim light that fought its way through the smoke-stained windows of a cantina. Painted in faded, crooked letters on one of the windowpanes was the name, *Tio's Mercantile and Cantina*.

The leather of our saddles squeaked as we dismounted and tied our horses to the hitch rail. There were four other horses standing three-legged at the rail. All wore Mexican-style saddles with large saddle horns and stirrups covered with tapaderos. Pulling our rifles from our scabbards, I followed Diego through the batwing doors.

On one side of the room were shelves stocked with a variance of merchandise; the other side served as the cantina. A thin layer of gray smoke clung to the low ceiling as the odors of whiskey and sweat mingled to stifle the air of the small building. The conversations quickly fell silent as we made our way toward a wooden plank resting atop two oak barrels that served as the bar. A poker game that had been in progress when we entered ceased as four Mexican men turned to study us with unfriendly eyes. Their sombreros were dusty, as were their clothes and the bullet-filled bandoliers across their chests, but the pistols they wore on their hips were not. I could feel their cold, hard stares burning holes in our backs as we bellied to the bar.

The Mexican bartender was a heavy-jowled man, his dingy white apron stained with the product of his occupation. I could see the reluctance in his movement as he hesitantly made his way down the short bar to where we stood.

After glancing at Diego his dark eyes uncomfortably held on mine. "*Senor*," he said, sounding apologetic, "I personally do not have a problem with your kind being here. But I must tell you there are others here that do."

"And what kind am I?" I asked, as I laid my Winchester on the scarred plank.

It was obvious he was nervous and uncomfortable. He looked to Diego for help. Diego stood silent, his expression unchanged.

"Well, uh … a *gringo*," he stammered.

He said *gringo* as though he was trying to disguise a cuss word. Sort of like putting lipstick on a pig, I surmised. I felt a smile cross my lips but there was no humor in the action. "Since we got our introductions out of the way and we're both confident that I'm a *gringo* and you're a Mexican, I believe I'll have a shot of whiskey. And bring my friend whatever he wants."

Perspiration beaded on the bartender's forehead as he looked to Diego. "The same," Diego said, his voice cold and hard.

Behind me, I heard the grating of chair legs on the wooden floor. In the reflection of a cracked mirror that hung behind the bar, I saw three of the men who had been sitting around the card table walking up behind us. Their spurs chimed with their steps. I could tell by their looks that this was not going to be a welcoming visit.

"*Amigo*," one of the men said. "Maybe you do not hear so well. We do not like your kind here."

Without turning around, I could see the reflection of three men in the mirror. The man doing the talking was the biggest of the three, his demeanor calloused and confident. I saw him turn toward the other two; a contemptuous smirk etched his dark face.

"Maybe the *gringo* is not deaf at all," he remarked to his companions. "Maybe he is just ignorant like the rest of them."

Reaching down, I picked up the shot glass in front of me and calmly took a sip. Setting the glass back down, I felt a stiff finger jab my shoulder. "I am talking to you, *cavarone*!"

Grabbing my Winchester by the barrel, I

quickly pivoted as I swung the rifle with both hands. The solid stock of the rifle cracked loud as it caught the man on the side of his head. The large sombrero he was wearing went flying across the small room as his legs went limp beneath him and he crumpled to the floor.

With amazing speed, Diego grabbed the man nearest him by the shirtfront and without so much as an effort sent him flying over the bar. I could hear glass shatter as the man slammed hard into the clouded mirror and fell to the floor. Shards of broken glass rained down on top of him.

The glint of a knife blade sliced through the air as I tried to recover my balance from swinging my rifle. I felt the searing burn of cold steel as the knife sliced across my forearm. The Mexican was poised for another swing of the knife when the cocking of Diego's rifle stilled the movement.

"*Alto! Ahora!*" Diego barked. "One more move and whatever you had for supper will have been your last!"

The Mexican, still holding the knife in a crouched stance, took a slight step backwards before glancing toward Diego. The knife showed a streak of red across the razor edge of the blade. The same red stain was coloring the sleeve of my shirt.

The man, still poised for another lunge, fidgeted anxiously as his eyes darted from Diego's gun to me. Even under the circumstances, it was obvious he was struggling with the decision of living or trying to kill me.

The fourth man, who had been sitting at the poker table, leisurely stood up. "That's enough, Juan. Put the knife away," he said with a wide, counterfeit grin. "That is no way to treat the guest of our friendly town."

I turned my rifle around as Juan backed away before reluctantly returning the knife to a sheath that hung from his belt.

"I am Roberto Salazar," the man said as he walked around from behind the table and approached the bar. "I must apologize for my friends here. I am not sure what came over them. They are usually men of peace and acceptance." His words dripped with rancid sarcasm.

The bartender, who had been crouching down behind the bar, slowly raised up. Reflected light sparkled on tiny fragments of glass that littered his shoulders.

"*Cantinero*," Salazar said to the bartender. "Set my friends up with a drink, *por favor*."

The bartender immediately grabbed a bottle from beneath the bar. His hands trembled as the whiskey he poured splashed onto the bar as much as it did into the two small glasses.

"I hope you will accept this as a token of my friendship," Salazar said as he stepped over the unconscious man that I had hit with my rifle butt.

I stood motionless as Diego, still holding his rifle in his right hand, reached for one of the glasses with his left. Picking up the glass, he raised it to his lips before pausing. Turning the glass upside down, he poured the contents on the face of the man lying in the floor.

"I think your peaceful friend here needs it more than we do," Diego said.

Salazar's black eyes turned murderous as a rivulet of sweat dripped from his stringy, unkempt hair. "*Amigo*, I believe what you have done is very disrespectful to me. Such an act is very, very foolish. Many men, much more capable than yourself, have died for much less reason than that," he said as he continued to study Diego.

Suddenly, I saw recognition show in the Mexican's face. "Ah, I know who you are," he nodded in satisfaction as he smiled and pointed a finger at Diego. "You must be Diego, the great big fool that searches for the phantom gold."

I could see Diego's finger tighten on the trigger of his rifle. I readied myself for the killings that seemed inevitable.

Roberto Salazar narrowed his eyes as he glanced at the rifles Diego and I held steady. Snapping his finger, he motioned to Juan to retrieve the man behind the bar. Digging the pointed toe of his boot into the ribs of the man lying on the floor until he slowly got up, Salazar continued. "Yes, I believe we will meet again real soon, Diego. And perhaps, on that occasion you and your *gringo* friend will not be holding a gun."

Diego's eyes were cold, his voice steely. "The

next time we meet, I will kill you like the mangy dog that you are."

The man smiled at Diego, his dingy, yellow teeth showing behind his grizzled beard. Salazar, following his men toward the doorway, stopped and turned around. "Tell your sister, I believe her name is Rosario, that I look forward to meeting her. I hear her beauty is second to none. I have a feeling she will get to know me very, very well," he scoffed before turning and disappearing through the swinging door.

I saw Diego stiffen at the comment. I walked to the doorway and cautiously watched as the men mounted their horses and rode slowly into the night. Rolling my sleeve above my forearm, I was relieved to see the knife wound was shallow, barely breaking the skin. Turning to face the bartender, I said, "Nice little town ya' have here. Is it always this friendly?"

The bartender shook his head. "*Senor* Salazar is a bad one," he said as he grabbed a broom and began sweeping the broken remnants of the mirror from the floor. "Since he came a couple of months ago with his men, the town trembles in fear at his presence. Many have left, but most are too poor to leave so they try to stay hidden when he is in town."

"How did he know my name and the name of my sister?" Diego asked.

The bartender shrugged his shoulders. "I do not know. *Senor* Salazar asks many questions and he gets his answers out of fear. Around here we call him the Butcher," he said as he reached behind the bar and picked up the long, spiny barb of a Yucca cactus and held it in front of us. An inch from the end of the sharp point was a horned toad, dead and half-eaten. "He got the name from a bird known as the Butcher Bird. This bird impales its prey on the sharp barbs of different plants so it can return to eat them at its leisure. With the bird this act is done not out of ruthlessness, but purely out of instincts. With Senor Salazar, this same brutal act is performed strictly for his pleasure. I would be very careful if I were you, *amigo*, for you have made a very bad enemy."

After finishing our drinks, we bought the supplies that we needed. With the horses packed and our rifles resting across the pommel of our saddles, we turned to leave when the bartender stepped through the doorway.

"*Senor*," he said as he looked to me. "There was a man here a couple of weeks ago asking of someone that fits your description."

"What did he look like?"

"He was a big man," he said, "riding a big black horse."

From the description, I instantly knew the man was John McCandle. My assumption had been right; McCandle was some type of law enforcement. Now he was on my trail, the same as the Ross's and the people of Clear Fork. My confidence waned, as I knew, without doubt, he was one man I did not want hunting me.

As we rode away the bartender called out, "May God ride with you."

In hopes of misleading any would-be pursuers, we headed west instead of north toward the mesa and the lost valley. The look on Diego's face was worried, much the same as I felt inside. I had no doubt the warning from the bartender about Roberto Salazar and his men was accurate and very real. Riding through the darkness, we stopped often to watch and listen for any unusual sounds that penetrated the night.

The sun had just crept above the eastern horizon the following morning before we stopped to rest our fatigued mounts. A wall of thunderheads was steadily gathering to the west as the early-morning air held a heaviness and carried a distant, but distinct smell of rain.

"That's the best thing we could hope for," I said as I watched the approaching clouds.

Diego, with a tired look on his face, glanced up from where he sat next to the horses. "What do you mean?"

"All we have to do is keep ridin' toward the storm. When we reach the edge of the rain we'll turn north and let the storm cover our tracks."

A slow grin spread across Diego's dark face. "You know," he said as he nodded, "even if you are a *gringo*, I'm starting to think you're all right."

"You might not be thinkin' that when we ride into the teeth of that storm," I said as I glanced up at the ever-darkening wall of clouds. "I've never known of any man with much smarts about him to intentionally go ride into an electrical storm out in the middle of the desert."

"A man has to do what a man has to do," Diego said nonchalantly. Lying back, he pulled his sombrero over his eyes and slept.

I continued to watch the dark, rolling storm clouds intensify as they billowed higher and higher above the barren landscape. Taking Diego's binoculars, I walked up a small rise several hundred yards from our camp. The storm, I figured, was still ten to twelve miles away and seemed to be slow-moving. The rain from the black clouds resembled a huge curtain as it fell in a slanted sheet toward the thirsting desert floor. Lightning spit haphazardly from the unsettled clouds. I carefully checked our back trail, but saw nothing. Leaning back against the warm surface of a large rock, I found myself giving into extreme exhaustion. I soon dozed off.

I awoke with a start as the first resounding clap of thunder rumbled across the desert floor. I did not know how long I had slept, but in that span of time the storm had moved noticeably closer. Turning the binoculars to the east, I jumped to my feet. No more than a mile away rode Roberto Salazar and ten of his men. They were riding hard, closing the distance fast.

Sprinting down the small slope, I called out to Diego, "Let's go! Salazar and his men are right behind us!"

Hastily tightening our cinches, we swung into our saddles and spurred hard. The mustangs responded, but I knew as leg-weary as they were, they would not be capable of doing so for long.

It was apparent within a couple of miles our worn mounts were no match for the fresher horses ridden by Salazar and his men. Turning my horse into the mouth of a ravine, Diego followed. The ravine was no more than ten feet wide and perhaps twenty feet high on the sides, but the sandy walls were steep. It was without doubt too steep for a horse to climb out of and probably even too steep for a man afoot to climb out of, as well. A steady trickle of water was snaking its way along the normally dry bottom of the rock-strewn draw. I knew we were in a bad situation, for the ravine ran to the northwest, acting as a funnel for the ireful storm clouds.

The labored breathing of our horses was loud as the first drops of stinging rain began pelting the ground around us. The black clouds boiled over us like waves in an angry sea. We continued to push our mounts hard as I desperately searched for a way out of the ravine. The water in the bottom of the draw quickly turned from a trickle to a deepening stream as water splashed high beneath the pounding hooves of our running horses. Glancing over my shoulder, I saw Salazar and his men suddenly come into view. A gun barked. The whining of a bullet zipped past my ear as the thunder rolled.

It became eerily dark before brilliant flashes of

lightning began stabbing at the ground over which we sped. Finally, I saw a way out of the creek bed as an intervening draw angled up and out. Turning into the ascending draw, I heard a horse squeal. Looking over my shoulder, I saw the lead rope ripped from Diego's hand as the packhorse he led tumbled to the ground as a bullet tore savagely through its side.

My horse was flagging as it attempted to scramble up the rain-slicked surface of the draw. Finally reaching the rim, I realized the mustang had no more to give. Turning loose of the packhorse, I grabbed my rifle as I leapt from the saddle. Diego rode past me before dismounting. Kneeling down next to me in what was now a torrential downpour, we held our rifles steady. Within seconds, Roberto Salazar and his men came splashing through the ever-deepening water in the ravine. As they attempted to turn into the angled draw, we met them with a barrage of deadly gunfire. With nowhere to retreat, they immediately returned fire. Instantly, three men riddled with bullets crumpled from the saddles of their panicked horses. The acrid smell of burnt gunpowder saturated the bullet-filled air.

A rumbling as loud as a locomotive suddenly resounded through the draw. I saw a terrified look crease Salazar's face as the ground beneath us began trembling an instant before a thunderous wall of water ripped through the narrow ravine. Screaming men and thrashing horses were tossed like tiny rag dolls as they were violently swept away. Where they had stood only seconds ago, now there was only brown, churning water ripping its way through the narrow ravine.

Diego and I, still kneeling and clutching our rifles, sat in stunned silence. After several minutes of staring at the turbulent water rushing past us, Diego looked over at me. When our eyes met, a slow grin began to crack his normally stoic features. Suddenly we began laughing as the rain continued to pour down upon us. Diego rolled to his back in the deepening mud as his bellowing laughter stifled the booming of the thunder. Even though the violent storm had been short-lived, the toll it exacted on Roberto Salazar and his men was fatally permanent.

After resting our horses for another day, we returned to the lone mesa. In spite of the loss of a good horse loaded with supplies, we both realized we had been extremely lucky, though neither of us said as much.

Rosario was anxiously awaiting our return as we entered the lost valley. With a smile touching her lips and her raven-black hair gently dancing in the breeze, she immediately ran to us as we rode up the narrow trail leading to the adobe. After hugging Diego, she quickly ran to me. Burying her head into my chest, I felt her arms clutch wantonly around my waist. Apprehensively, I allowed my arms to drop to her shoulders. I could no longer fight my desires as I tightly wrapped both my arms around her and held her securely to my body.

A wave of peacefulness that I had not known for such a long time swept over me as we stood holding each other. With Rosa clutched in my arms it was as though all of my troubles somehow seemed to dissipate in the distance of my past.

It was a fleeting feeling as reality burrowed its way back into my thoughts. Stepping back, I held her at arms length. "It's nice to see ya'," I said as I nodded. "You look more beautiful than ever."

I could see the look of disappointment on her face as her brown eyes probed deep into mine. A thin smile finally parted her lips. "Thank you," she whispered. "You look very beautiful to me as well."

I smiled before turning away. I had the feeling that Rosa was desperately trying to remove the wall that surrounded me, one brick at a time, hoping, that with the removal of enough bricks, the powerful wall would one day weaken and come tumbling down. As I began unloading the packhorse, Rosa returned to the adobe. I watched her depart as the long white dress she wore swished enticingly with the movement of her hips.

I felt Diego's eyes on me as he uncinched the saddle from his horse. "Maybe," he said, "you should reconsider your decision."

After lowering the pack to the ground, I straightened up. "What do ya' mean?"

Diego shrugged. "It is very obvious, is it not? Rosario has a very deep love for you. Maybe you should consider changing your plans."

How a man changes what burns inside of him, I did not know. "I know from watching you that you haven't been able to change what drives you, and neither could your father. What makes you think I'm any different?"

"I'm not saying you are any different. I'm just saying that if I had the love of a beautiful woman, such as Rosario, that maybe I would reconsider. To have the love of someone as pure and genuine as her is more opportunity than most men will ever know in their lifetime."

I shook my head as I stripped my saddle from the mustang. What Diego said I knew was true but it was not an option in my life, such as it was. I did not want to continue the conversation, so I let it drop.

That evening as the sun slowly began to disappear, I found myself setting high upon the canyon rim staring off to the northeast, the direction of Clear Fork. The desert air was cooling as long dark shadows inched silently across the desiccated land. For someone like myself, who had been raised in Tennessee, a land filled with trees and streams, I had over time grown to appreciate the surreal beauty of the desert. The vastness and non-forgiving nature it posed had a way of humbling even the strongest man.

In the following days, as Diego and I attacked boulders in yet another cave; I felt a growing restlessness building within me. To stay much longer, even though that is what I wished more than anything, was only serving as a form of torment for myself and more importantly it was tormenting for Rosa as well. I knew my time to leave was drawing nearer with each passing day.

The pounding of our sledges rang loudly as they struck the surface of the boulders. I could tell by the curvature of the back wall that we were once again nearing the end of another of the many caves.

Setting my double jack aside, I sat down on one of the rocks we had cleared away. "Diego, we need to talk."

Diego took one more swing before he turned and faced me. "What is it, *amigo?*"

I sat a moment, staring at the rubble that surrounded us. "Diego, it's time for me to go."

His dark face was expressionless as he sat down next to me. I could tell by the look in his black eyes that he was deep in thought before he spoke. "I'll be honest with you, amigo, I think you are making a very big mistake. It is sad to say, but as well you already know, it is a mistake that cannot be undone."

I did not respond at first as I sat staring ahead. He was not telling me anything that I did not know already. It was the same thing that I had been telling myself ever since my eyes first touched on the beauty of Rosario Cruz. In the time I had spent in the lost mesa I had grown to admire Diego, even with his obsession of the lost gold that to me seemed lacking in good judgment. However, over that same period of time I knew I had grown to love Rosa.

"I have never said such a thing," he said before pausing to bend over and pick up a small sliver of shattered rock, "because I have never known a man that I felt deserving. With you, it is different. I wish you would marry Rosa and take her away from here. This is my life … it is not hers. She deserves much more than this."

I felt guilt inside of me, knowing that if only I could somehow change my life I could change hers as well. It was a futile thought, for I knew I could not. As I sat thinking, my eyes casually examined the pile of rocks before us. Suddenly I sat up straight. "Diego, look!"

Diego glanced over at me before his eyes followed my pointing finger. Peaking from beneath a boulder in front of us was what appeared to be a worn piece of burlap sacking. Diego slowly sank down to his knees next to the boulder. With his eyes wide, he tentatively reached for the tattered burlap as though he was afraid it was not really there. When at last his fingers touched the cloth, I saw his whole body tremble.

"It is here," he whispered as he gently caressed the material in the palm of his hand. "It is here."

Quickly we began removing the remainder of the rubble. Partway buried beneath the sandy floor of the cave lay the fabled gold of Jose De La Vasquez and his Spanish Conquistadors. The gold had been crudely smelted into bars each weighing what I figured to be about twenty-five pounds. By the end of the day, neatly stacked before us were a hundred–and twenty bricks of pure gold.

"Now what?" I asked as I looked at Diego.

Diego's reaction to the newly found wealth was not what I would have expected. Instead of being beside himself with the discovery, his mood was solemn and reserved.

He did not respond to my question, he just sat staring with a nondescript look on his face. His dark eyes were transfixed on the gold but I could tell his thoughts were elsewhere. I knew he had always believed in the gold but after all the years spent searching, between him and his father, uncertainty somewhere along the way had to have slowly crept into his mind.

I figured it was much like a poker game where in the beginning you felt you were dealt the best hand at the table. However, after numerous raises and re-raises you began to doubt that belief, but you realized you were in too deep to back out so you pushed the last of your life savings into the pot. All that was left afterwards was turning your cards face up and living with the consequences. I had no doubt that over the years Diego had not only pushed his whole life into the pot, he had gambled his soul as well. As it turned out, he had held the winning cards in his hands all along.

Diego leaned over, picked up one of the gold bars and cradled it in his hands much the way a mother would cradle a newborn child. "I suppose it is time for me to live up to my promise." With an obvious reluctance, he carefully placed the gold brick back on top of the stack. "I promised Rosa many years ago that when I found the lost treasure we would go to Santa Fe to live. After all the years she has sacrificed her own life in this valley, for my father and then for me, that is all she ever asked for in return."

"She'll be happy," I said.

Diego nodded his agreement. "I will be leaving before first light to go recruit the help of my uncle. He is the youngest of my father's six brothers and the only one that did not think my father a fool. His loyalty to my father, as well as to me, will be richly rewarded." The satisfaction was apparent in Diego's eyes.

"Do you want me to come with you?" I asked.

Diego shook his head. "No, my friend. You stay here with Rosa. I will return in a couple of days."

The morning following Diego's departure, I was sitting next to the small stream when I saw Rosa walking down the narrow, winding trail toward me. Her black hair, unbraided, was down around her shoulders, lightly swaying with her graceful movements. Our eyes met as she sat down in the tall grass next to me. A smile touched her lips as she reached over and placed a hand on my arm.

"I guess Diego told you?" I asked.

She nodded her head as her fingers gently squeezed my arm. "Yes," she whispered. "He told me of the gold."

"I'm happy for both of ya'," I said. "You've seen your dreams come true."

The smile slowly faded from her lips as she gazed across the valley, the wind softly playing with her hair. "I suppose a dream is sometimes a fleeting thing," she said. "It seems one can have the same dream for such a long time, and then, in no more than the blink of an eye, something happens to change that dream. Sometimes I think dreams are meant to be that, just a dream."

Moving closer, she rested her head on my shoulder. I could feel the softness of her hair against the side of my cheek as she nestled snuggly against me. Taking her hand in mine, we sat silently, staring off into the distance. I think both of us were desperately trying to somehow see a future for us, but it was a future that was not there.

When she again spoke, her voice was touched with sadness. "Diego said that soon you would be leaving us."

"Yes," I replied. "It's time for me to go."

Rosa moved around in front of me, sitting with her knees bent beneath her. She took my hands in hers and clutched them to her chest. I could see tears welling up in her brown eyes.

"Don't cry," I whispered. I wiped away a tear that had spilled onto her cheek. "It's just the way it has to be."

"I don't know how I can possibly live without

you. Is there nothing I can do to make you want me?" she asked as her eyes searched deep into mine. "I love you, Chance Tucker. Is there nothing I can do to make you love me back?"

I wanted so desperately to tell her that I did love her and that I wanted her more than she could possibly imagine. But I knew I could not. I gently pulled her into my arms and held her tight to my body. I felt her warm tears on the side of my face; her body softly trembled as she wept. A lone cloud slowly drifted across the face of the sun, sending a fleeting shadow dancing across the valley floor where we sat.

Neither of us spoke as we lay in each other's arms. It was as though our bodies and souls melted together, extracting every ounce of comfort the other had to offer. The fading sun splashed the sky above us with weakening rays of pinks and reds before Rosa reluctantly stood up. Bending down, she kissed my cheek before silently walking away.

Sitting alone in the tall grass next to the clear stream, I listened to the water spilling softly over the bordering rocks of the pond before continuing its winding path through the fertile valley. Next to me, the long, supple branches of a willow tree gently swayed back and forth with the light breeze that whispered through the basin. I watched as the herd of mustangs grazed peacefully on the green grass while several goats effortlessly traversed the steep, rocky walls of the surrounding cliffs. This is what peace could truly be like,

I thought to myself. I bowed my head, for I knew this was only the calm before the inevitable storm that was methodically brewing in the town of Clear Fork and in my life.

CHAPTER 12

The following day, I sat high upon the wall of the mesa as Diego rode into the valley. A half dozen Mexican men rode with him, leading a string of burros and four mules. Each of the burros carried a sawbuck packsaddle with empty, canvas panniers on their back. The four mules bore the sweaty outline of a harness on their slick coats.

The men followed single file down the rocky path, their heads appearing to be on swivels as they took in the beauty of the lost valley for the first time. Diego, riding past the trail that angled toward the adobe, led the men to a clearing next to the small stream before stepping from his saddle. The men immediately dismounted and stripped their saddles from their mounts before allowing the stock to water.

Within minutes I saw Diego, accompanied by another, leave the gathered men and begin walking toward the adobe. As they neared the dwelling, Rosario rushed from the house into the man's outstretched arms. I assumed the man to be the uncle Diego had previously spoken of, the youngest brother to his father.

After watching the three retreat inside, I carefully worked my way around the rim of the canyon. Nearing the entrance to the mesa, I peered over the outer edge of the cliff. On the floor of the desert sat a wagon. In the bed of the wagon were four wooden barrels, I assumed their purpose to be for transporting water. I realized the wagon had been left outside the mesa as it was too wide to pass through the narrow passageway into the valley. The presence of the wagon and harness, however, explained the sweat marks on the mules I had observed earlier.

Being after midday, I figured the loading of the gold and the start of the excursion to Santa Fe would not begin today. However, knowing Diego was not the type of man to set idle for long, I had no doubt tomorrow morning would be the beginning.

The cool of the evening had begun to set in before I walked the trail off the rim and into the basin. Shadows were lying across the valley floor as I knocked on the door of the adobe.

I was met by Rosa. "Chance, you don't have to knock."

"Well, I didn't want to interrupt anything."

"Don't be silly," she said as she reached for my arm and guided me inside.

Diego stood up from the table, as did the

Mexican man beside him. "Chance, this is my uncle, Ignacio Cruz," Diego said. "He has come to help with the journey to Santa Fe."

There was a noticeable resemblance in the man's hard features and intense eyes. He was not as tall as Diego, but he was built stout and solid.

"Chance Tucker," I said as I extended my hand. "Nice to meet ya', sir."

There seemed to be a reluctance in the man's dark eyes as he studied me before reaching out and shaking my hand. His grip was not only firm, but firm to the point I felt as if he were attempting to send me some sort of message. An ire quickly rose in me. What message he intended to express I did not know, nor did I care.

"Chance, please sit down," Rosa said as she slid a chair from underneath the table.

"I have a few things I need to do," I said. The bluntness of my reply came out more so than I had intended. "Thank you, anyway."

I didn't know what problem the man had with me. However, one thing I did know, I had a hell of a lot more important things to think about than him. I hoped for Rosa and Diego's sake that it was not too obvious that I did not really care to be in the same room with Ignacio. I glimpsed the look of disappointment on Rosa's face as I nodded and stepped out the door.

Walking down the pathway to where I had been sleeping at night, I sat down next to the stream.

Pulling my Winchester from the saddle scabbard, I began wiping the rifle down. Even though I knew it was irrelevant, I kept trying to make sense of Ignacio's cold reaction to me. I had told Diego, after the discovery of the gold, that I would only ride with them part of the way to Santa Fe. Once we entered into New Mexico, I would be turning north and heading in the direction of Clear Fork.

Returning the cleaned rifle to its leather case, I decided the best thing to do during that interim period would be to stay as far away from Ignacio and the other men as possible.

Farther down the stream, I could hear talking and laughter as the group of men who had returned with Diego were busily making their camp. As dusk gave way to night, the soft glow of their fire shimmered off the dark sky above. Before long, the faint smell of burning mesquite drifted throughout the valley.

Making a small fire of my own, I put a pot of coffee on to boil. It was not long before the water in the blackened pot began to hiss and sputter. I was squatting on my heels pouring myself a cup when Diego and Ignacio came walking down the path from the adobe toward me. I stood up before taking a sip of the hot coffee.

As the two men approached, Diego said, "My friend, tonight is not the night to drink coffee. Tonight is the night for tequila. It is a night to celebrate."

I smiled at Diego. When I glanced over at

Ignacio, he stood staring at me, his black eyes expressionless. Tequila was not my drink of choice, but when Diego extended the bottle, I took it. I did not want my demeanor to dampen his spirits on such a special occasion for him. Tilting the bottle up, I took a swig. The fiery liquid burned all the way down my throat and into the pit of my stomach. When the burning finally fizzled out, all that was left was the lingering aftertaste.

"Ignacio, go on ahead," Diego said as he placed his hand on his uncle's shoulder. "I will be along shortly."

Ignacio gave me a sideways glance before turning and heading down the path in the direction of the other camp.

As we stood looking at each other across the fire, I could tell by the redness in Diego's eyes he had started the celebration earlier in the day. In those same glassy eyes, I could see that something was troubling him.

"There is something I must show you," Diego said. Reaching into his shirt pocket, he retrieved a crinkled piece of paper. After carefully unfolding the paper and somewhat smoothing the wrinkles, he handed it to me. With the paper in my hand, I stepped closer to the light of the fire. My eyes carefully scanned the paper in the dim light.

I shook my head as I took a deep breath. "Well, that explains a few things," I acknowledged. "I knew somethin' didn't seem right but I couldn't figure out what it was."

"My uncle is the only one of the men who has seen you up close," he commented. "Even though I explained the situation to him, he still remains skeptical. I am giving my uncle one-tenth of the gold, which is a very large sum. But the price on the wanted poster of two thousand dollars for you, dead or alive, is much more than I am paying the men who came with him. I do not know these other men well and according to what my uncle has said, they all have seen the poster."

Staring into my cup, I swished the coffee around in a smooth circle before pouring it out on the ground. Suddenly, even the coffee seemed to taste bitter.

"All of these men," Diego continued, "are very poor as we all have been in our lives. With the offer I have made them for their services they will make more money in the next two weeks then they have made in ten years. But, two thousand dollars is probably more money then they will make in their entire lifetime. What they might do if they recognize you, I do not know."

I carefully looked at the poster again. There was no mistaking the likeness on the paper. If Ignacio had recognized me immediately, I had no doubt the others would as well. "Diego, you need these men's help to get the gold to Santa Fe. This shipment is too valuable to do it any other way. Maybe it'd be best for everyone if I throw my belongin's together and head out tonight."

I handed the wanted dodger back to Diego as I waited for his response. We stood in silence. The only sound was the popping of the mesquite wood in the small fire.

Diego took another pull on the bottle before he spoke. "I have come to know, even with the color of our skin being different; we are very much the same kind of man. I have seen this in the way we do things ... and in the way we think," he said as he glanced across the fire at me. Crumpling the paper in his hands, he let it fall into the flames of the fire. The fire quickly consumed the paper, leaving only the ash to stir in the light breeze.

"It is true, the gold is very valuable," he continued. "But it is not more valuable than a true friend. I will stand by you the same as you stood by your friend, Tig."

I let his words sink in as I stared into the golden flames of the fire. "Is there anything I can say to change your mind?"

He smiled. "My friend, you know me better than that. We both, unfortunately, have the hard head of a bull. If you do not believe this," he added as he again uncorked the bottle, "ask Rosa. She will tell you."

I could do nothing but agree with his statement as he again passed the bottle to me. Much to my disappointment, the second drink tasted no better than the first.

It was not long before Diego headed down the

trail to the other camp and I stood alone in the flickering shadows of my fire. Squatting down, I poked at the dying embers with a stick. It seemed with the people of Clear Fork watching for me and John McCandle scouring the countryside for my whereabouts and now the possibility of the men, who are now in this same valley as I, recognizing me and turning me in for the reward money, my chances of avenging Tig's death were growing dimmer with each passing minute.

I disgustedly stood up and tossed the small stick into the fire. One fact I was certain of … I would not be taken alive. And if that time came, there would be plenty of blood from others spilled on the ground next to mine.

Picking up my bedroll, I smoothed it out on the ground next to the stream and lay atop of it. It was a moonless night, the stars gleaming crisp and bright against the backdrop of the black sky. I lay in troubled thought as the water from the streamed trickled past.

Suddenly, I came to my feet. Grabbing my bridle, I headed through the trees in search of the horse herd. I found the mustangs grazing at the far end of the valley. I spoke to them softly as their eyes sought me out in the darkness. Their heads were held high on stiff necks, their ears pricked forward.

"Easy now," I whispered as I walked closer. The reassurance of my voice calmed the anxiety of their natural instincts. They returned to cropping grass as I quietly milled through the herd. When I found the gelding I had ridden to San Ramon, I slipped the bridle over its head. Taking the reins, I led him away from the other horses.

Nearing my camp, I tied the mustang out of sight in the deep shadows. Quickly gathering my belongings and filling my canteen, I threw my saddle on the horse. With my gear packed and ready, I retrieved my diary from my saddlebags. Tearing a page from the back of the small book, I wrote a short note and placed it in the fork of a tree next to my fire.

I stood listening a moment before I swung into the saddle and headed toward the opening in the mesa. Other than the occasional sound of my horse's hooves striking a stone or the squeak of my saddle, the night lay quite as I made my way down the path.

Nearing the trail that led to the adobe, I paused. With the curtains pulled back from the windows and the glow of candles lighting the room, I saw Rosa sitting at the table. Her black hair was pulled tight in a braid that fell over her shoulder and shined brightly in the soft light. Her face was calm and beautiful.

"I love you," I whispered. Touching my spurs to the ribs of the mustang, I quietly rode away.

Once outside the confines of the mesa, I pulled my horse to a halt and watched as a full moon began to peek over the desolate horizon. With the slow ascent of the moon, the desert seemed to come to life with the expectant arrival. The white sand gradually became fluorescent, giving definition to each individual rock and cactus that appeared to stretch into a distant eternity.

With one last look over my shoulder at the mesa that held the beautiful lost valley isolated, yet secure in its bosom, I squeezed my horse into a trot heading east.

In the time I had spent with Diego, he taught me much of surviving in the harsh element into which I rode. With a lifetime spent in the desert, he had learned many of the idiosyncrasies by which it lived and breathed. He had come to know the desert, not only as a place, but also as a brother. The knowledge of dependable water holes, which were few and far between, he passed on to me.

The ground beneath the mustang passed quickly and quietly beneath its hooves. With only brief pauses to rest my horse, I rode throughout the night. The stars were beginning to fade and the sky was turning pink as I saw in the near distance one of the landmarks of which Diego had spoken.

An outcropping of rocks jutted from the face of a small, sandy rise. As we weaved through the maze of prickly pear cactus in the direction of the rocks, the mustang raised its head and flared its nostrils. He undoubtedly smelled water.

At the base of the rocks seeped a pool of water. The seep was small, not much larger in diameter than a washtub, and it smelled of sulfur. Although the water was laden with alkali and had a discernable odor, it was drinkable. I allowed the mustang to drink only a small amount, just enough to get him through until we found something more sustaining. I took a swallow from my canteen as I looked into the distance. From what Diego had told me, the next water was close to fifty miles away. At that waterhole, he said the water was not only sweet and plentiful but there would be grass for my horse, as well. I allowed the horse to rest awhile as I crawled into the shade of the rocks and closed my eyes. Sleep quietly settled over me.

When I awoke, I allowed the mustang another shallow drink before I mounted and began the search for the next landmark. The day was not hot; it was just warm enough to allow a cooling sweat to accumulate on my clothes and on the skin of the mustang.

Even though the desert had nearly claimed my life on my last excursion across its unstaked but guarded territory, I had come to have great respect and appreciation for its truthfulness. With the desert there was nothing hidden. It lay naked and unashamed before each man who neared it, with no false perceptions, no promises and no guarantees of survival. It was neither beckoning nor shunning. It was just there.

As I rode across the face of the glimmering sand, I harbored no doubts the world would be a much better place if only men could live that way as well. I knew from personal experience they could not, nor would they ever.

I was lost in my thoughts when I first felt what

I thought was a slight limp in my horse's forefoot on the offside. Dismounting, I picked up the foot. There was no visible mark but when I pressed on the sole of the foot I saw a twitch in the muscles of his shoulder. The foot was tender. Kneeling down, I wrapped my hands around the ankle. There was without doubt a slight heat. I knew the mustang had a stone bruise that was not yet visible on the surface. In most cases, a bruise such as this would heal itself with time. However, I also knew it would continue to worsen carrying my weight on its back.

"Nothin' is ever easy, is it boy?" I said, disgruntled as I patted the mustang on its shoulder. "Well, I do know one thing. We ain't gonna get there as long as we're standing here."

Taking the reins in my hand, we began walking. I figured the next watering hole was still between twelve to fifteen very long miles away.

CHAPTER 13

The night had long set in before I entered into a remote mott of mesquites that huddled closely together in the narrow funnel of a shallow draw. It was as Diego said; the water was cool and plentiful. A carpet of green grass crowded the banks of the life-sustaining liquid.

The limp of the mustang had grown noticeably worse with the long trek. After stripping the saddle and gear from its back, I led it out into the shallow pool of water. I hoped the coolness of the water would help draw some of the heat away from the bruised hoof. With Clear Fork remaining in the far distance, I had no choice but to wait whatever length of time it took for the horse to heal. I was hoping it would be no more than three or four days, but I knew it could very well be longer.

After a half hour, I led the horse from the water and staked it out to graze. Gathering a handful of dried sticks, I built a small fire and placed the blackened coffeepot in the edge of the flames. Rummaging through my saddlebags, I grabbed a piece of jerked beef. Having left in the night the way I did, I had no time to procure any rations. Once the few remaining pieces of jerky were gone, meals would be meager if anything at all.

As I sat drinking a cup of coffee and trying to satisfy the grumbling of my stomach, I reiterated my earlier thought: the desert makes no promises.

In the faint light of the fire I could see numerous fresh tracks of small game around the water. With me camping where I was, most animals would avoid the water unless desperation overrode their fear of my presence. That could be a long time. And if there happened to be another source of water in the area, it could be until after I vacated the area completely. I sat enviously listening to the horse chew the blades of the filling grass.

When the sun rises tomorrow it would give me a chance to survey the area. With any luck there would be somewhere close I could hole up a short distance away in hopes of getting a shot at something coming in to the spring to drink.

Depending on how fast the mustang healed, there was a distinct possibility that I would still be here when Diego and Rosa passed through with the gold. If that turned out to be the case, I would be right back where I started from, with the fear of being recognized by the men with them.

Life is always filled with twists and turns. However, it sure seems as of late my life had been filled with nothing but steep and dangerous switchbacks. Until tomorrow there was nothing more I could do about my situation, so I spread my bedroll and slept.

The morning's sun found me searching the area on foot. A half-mile to the north I found another small grove of trees. When I got closer, I saw where a seep had recently held water but was now dry. However, grass still surrounded the muddy depression in the ground. I hated to force the mustang to walk that far away but moving away from the spring would offer me the best chance of finding some kind of game to kill.

After moving the horse to the dry seep and staking it out on the grass, I crept back down toward the spring and lay in wait atop a small rise that overlooked the thicket of mesquites. The wait was long but my hopes were high as I patiently watched. The shadows were growing long and the cool of the evening was drifting across the face of the desert before I raised my rifle and squeezed the trigger.

After collecting my kill, I hurried back to the new camp. The mustang, uneasy at the smell of blood, raised its head and nervously snorted as I approached. Quickly kindling a fire, I anxiously awaited as the meat began to blacken on the end of a sharpened stick. The mustang, with a full belly, watched me with a heightened curiosity.

"What are you lookin' at?" I mumbled around a

bite of the blackened meat. "Ain't ya' ever seen anybody eat coyote before?"

Three days slowly passed as I watched the mustang grow sounder. Even though the tenderness caused by the stone bruise was lessening, the horse was not yet fit enough to carry me to Clear Fork. Therefore, I continued to wait and subsist on whatever creature sought out the water of the spring. It was while laying atop the small rise one evening, patiently awaiting my next meal, that I noticed a tendril of dust rising above the desert floor to the west. It was not long before the mule-drawn wagon and the gold-laden burros, trudging along heavy-footedly through the soft sand, came into view. Their steps were strained and deliberate under the heavy burden they carried.

I felt a sudden excitement filter throughout my body. I was not at all anxious to see the men who rode with Diego, but I eagerly anticipated being near Rosa once again. The possibility of being recognized, which I had sought to escape from in the lost valley, now not only seemed probable but eminent.

I thought of staying out of sight at the other camp but I had been having to lead the mustang to the spring every morning and evening to drink. I figured I could make the horse do without water for a day or so and wait for their departure. However, I had no way of knowing how long they would stay. There was a good chance they would allow the animals to rest and graze for several days.

I decided I would just have to take my chances and hope I was not recognized. I got to my knees and prepared to stand before I quickly dropped back down to my stomach. Something did not look right. What was it? I kept watching above the crest of the rise as the caravan crept nearer. It struck me swift and hard. Diego was not on horseback; he was in the bed of the wagon. Alongside of him sat Rosa and their uncle, Ignacio. My heart began beating rapidly. Something was wrong. Terribly wrong.

I inched down the backside of the small rise and lay on my back out of sight. My mind was racing wildly, trying to make sense of the situation. The only conclusion I could draw was the five Mexican men who Diego had hired to help move the gold had taken control of the bullion.

It was not long before the caravan drew into the edge of the mesquites that surrounded the spring. Where I lay hidden was no more than a hundred yards away. My fears were quickly substantiated as I watched Diego, Rosa and Ignacio stiffly step down from the bed of the wagon under gunpoint. It was plain to see that Diego's hands were tied behind his back, as were Ignacio's. Even from that distance, I could see that Diego was limping noticeably, his face battered and streaked with dried blood. As I watched the captors milling around the stream, I worried about my own detection. Even with the wind constantly shifting the surface of the sand, the tracks that had been left in my comings and goings were still faintly visible.

Being out hunting as I was, I only had my rifle at my side. My pistol had been left behind. In order to have a chance of helping Diego and Rosa I knew I had to get back to my camp. The path between the two was sparse and open. There was no way I could make it in the daylight without being seen. I would have to wait until dark.

It was not long before the mules were unharnessed and the burros were unpacked and led to water. A trail of black smoke soon lifted amidst the trees and dissipated into the sky. When the sky darkened, I crouched low and hurried to my camp.

Taking a thin piece of leather, I tied it between the end of the lead rope and the picket pin. "Just in case I don't make it back," I said as I patted the horse on its shoulder. "You won't have any trouble breaking that."

Grabbing my pistol, I worked my way back toward the spring. I had to get a gun to Diego and Ignacio. There was no other way. I would not have a chance against five armed men. Crawling closer, I could hear talking and laughter above the popping of the fire.

As I neared, I could see, with the reflection of the fire, four of the men. Where was the other? Was he standing watch away from the camp? And if so, where was he? If I gave my Winchester to Diego and my pistol to Ignacio, I would have to locate the other man with only a knife in my possession. If we attacked the others first, we would come under fire from the dark. It would be almost guaranteed there would be casualties among us. With Rosa's presence, I could not take that chance. I had to locate the fifth man first.

I was so close to Rosa I could hear her soft sobs. I wanted to tell her that I was here and that I would somehow make things better. I only hoped it would be true. I slowly inched my way back away from the camp and into the darkness. The moon, which would be bright, had not yet risen. I had to find the man before then or I would stand out against the white sand like a snake in the middle of a cobblestone road. I sat in the dark frantically searching the night. It was not until the glow of a cigarette penetrated the dark that I was able to pinpoint his location. He was no more than fifty yards from the spring but on the opposite side from where I lay hidden. He had to be facing the camp or I would not have seen the glow from the cigarette. I knew I would have to skirt completely around him in order to sneak up on him from behind.

I could feel my heart thumping against my chest harder and faster the closer I came. If I failed, I knew we would all be killed. I was within ten yards of the unsuspecting man before his silhouette appeared like an apparition. His back was to me. I saw his hand lower before sparks from his flicked cigarette showered to the ground. I heard him grumble as he peered down at the cherry that had fallen from the end of the smoke with the action and lay smoldering on the sand.

I laid my rifle to my side and pulled my knife from my scabbard as I rose to a crouching position. The sand was silent beneath my feet as I took one cautious step and paused before taking another. He had just struck a match on the seat of his britches when I grabbed him from behind. My left hand clamped tight over his mouth as I drove the knife blade into his back. I held his body with all my strength as I continued to plunge the blade of the knife repeatedly into his back. The rifle slipped from his fingers as his body went limp in my arms. I slowly lowered him to the ground, continuing to hold my hand over his mouth until he drew his last breath and lay silent in the sand. His unseeing eyes began to shine like obsidian as the moon peeked above the horizon.

Grabbing the man's rifle as well as my own, I began carefully crawling back around to the other side of the camp. I felt an urgency rising with the moon as the fluorescent sand began to glow around me. I knew that if any of the men wandered away from the spindly grove of mesquites and the glow of the fire, I would stand out like a white man in Santa Anna's Mexican army. I immediately began crawling as fast as my knees and elbows would carry me.

I breathed a quiet sigh of relief as I found refuge in the scant shadows of the trees. I paused to catch my breath before I eased behind Diego. "Just hold still," I whispered as I slid my knife against the ropes that bound his wrists. The rope frayed and separated. I eased the butt of the dead man's rifle into his hand. "Wait until I move Rosa out of the way." I saw a slight acknowledging nod of his head. Moving behind Ignacio I repeated the procedure, before placing my pistol in his grasp.

I saw Rosa flinch as my voice startled her. "Be real still," I whispered before I cut the ropes from her hands. "I'm gonna jerk you out of the way."

Soon as she nodded her head, I yanked her backwards with my left hand. She gasped as she hit the ground on her back. I saw the startled men instantly spin on their heels as they grabbed for their pistols holstered on their hips. I was bringing my rifle level when Diego's rifle shattered the stillness, and then Ignacio's followed. The small confined area erupted into a barrage of gunfire. I was working the lever on my Winchester furiously as bullets ripped through the trees around me.

I saw two of the men crumple to the ground, and then a third. My face seemed to catch fire and my eyes suddenly went blurry as the bark of a mesquite tree splintered into my face. I heard Ignacio let out a loud moan and then I felt him fall against my leg. I was still firing as I tried to blink my eyes clear. Through watery eyes, I saw the last man stumble awkwardly toward us, his gun firing into the ground in front of him. I heard Diego's rifle boom one final time as the man's head seemed to explode. The man sank to his knees before pitching face first into the spring. In the firelight, I could see the water gradually turn red around him.

I quickly turned to Rosa. "Are you okay?" I asked as I helped her to her feet. She was white as a ghost and could only nod before falling into my arms.

Ignacio slowly rose to his feet, wincing in pain as he clutched his shoulder. "Are you hit hard?" I asked.

"No," he grimaced. "Not too hard, I think."

Diego's face was fixed hard, his eyes riveted on the bodies of the dead men. I watched as he walked over to the man lying in the stream and grabbed him by his boots. The man was still face down as Diego dragged him from the stream and toward the perimeter of the spindly trees. A trail of blood and gore followed the man out of sight. I held Rosa clutched to my chest so she would not see. I knew she had already seen more than any woman should.

I held her until I felt her fear slowly subside. "You should tend to your uncle," I said. She nodded before going to his side.

While Rosa cleaned and bandaged her uncle's wound, Diego and I began dragging the remainder of the bodies away from the spring. The task was unpleasant to me but Diego seemed indifferent to it all. It was as though he were dragging dead skunks away from a henhouse.

As we dragged the last body, the body of the man I had killed on the outskirts of the camp, I said,

"I'll go get a shovel so we can bury 'em."

When I started to turn I felt Diego's powerful hand grip my arm. "That is not necessary," he said bluntly.

"You don't want to bury 'em?"

"I would not cheat the buzzards," he said, expressionless. "The birds deserve better than that … the thieves do not."

We remained at the spring two more days. On the morning of the third day, we pulled out at daybreak. Ignacio, under Rosa's protest, drove the wagon one-handed, his left shoulder bound tightly to his chest. I smiled as I listened to the berating Rosa was giving her uncle. He stared straight ahead as though he did not hear. Rosa, sitting next to him on the wagon seat, soon gave up and sat in silence. I could plainly see the stubborn family trait that had evidently filtered down through the generations. I guess I really had no room to talk, that would be sort of like the pot calling the kettle black.

Diego, again on horseback, rode behind the wagon leading the six burros loaded with the gold. I rode beside him leading the four horses, which were now extras. One horse had been killed at the springs by a stray bullet during the gunfire. The mustang beneath me, fully recovered from the stone–bruise, was well rested. He tugged at the bit, displaying his impatience at the slow pace at which we were forced to travel.

As we made our way across the desert, my eyes were constantly drawn to Rosa. Even with the swirling dust laying on her hair and clothing she was the most beautiful woman I had ever seen. In the evenings, when camped, we talked. However, the conversations were of a general topic, not of the past nor of the future. With great struggle, our true feelings were kept silent, secured away in the depths of our own thoughts.

Every once in a while I would feel Diego's eyes on me and I would immediately avert my gaze from Rosa. Finally, he leaned to me and said in a low voice, "It is not too late, amigo. It is only too late when we allow it to be so."

"I wish that were true," I replied solemnly. "I wish that were true."

After traveling seven days from the spring, Santa Fe came into view. The peaks of the surrounding Sangre de Cristo mountains had been painted white with an early fall snow, but the town lay in the warmth of the valley below.

Ignacio looked over his shoulder at me and I nodded my head. He pulled the mules to a halt. I stepped from the saddle, as did Diego. Rosa and Ignacio climbed down from the seat as I secured the lead rope of the horses I had been leading to the back of the wagon. We stood in an uncomfortable silence, no one seeming to know what to say.

Finally Ignacio spoke. "Travel safe," he said as he extended is hand. "And thank you." I shook his hand before he turned and climbed back atop the wagon seat.

I saw Rosa's body softly tremble as tears began spilling from her dark eyes and onto her cheeks. Reaching out, I pulled her into my arms and held her tight against me. A southern breeze gently played with her silky hair as the warmness of her tears soaked into the fabric of my shirt. I could feel my heart breaking as the innocence of her body continued to melt into my arms. She had never felt so frail and vulnerable to me as she did now. A sadness that was beyond any I thought possible tore savagely at my heart. I clinched my jaws tight as I defiantly fought away the unwanted emotions and the tears that threatened my eyes.

When Rosa felt my body stiffen, she dejectedly pulled away from my arms. Her delicate shoulders straightened before she raised her chin, her eyes searching deep into mine. "I love you," she whispered as the tears on her cheeks glistened in the sunlight. "It should not be your time to die."

I desperately searched for comforting words, words that could somehow sooth the pain I saw in her, but I found none. Standing silent, I felt the warmth of her lips as she reached up and kissed my cheek before turning away. As I watched her walk to the front of the wagon, I saw in her the delicate petal of a beautiful rose that was beginning to wither after being touched by the frost of an early morning.

I felt Diego's hand on my shoulder. "We will

miss, you, my friend."

We clasped our arms around each other. "I will miss you both as well." As he started to turn away I said, "Tell Rosa that … " I left the sentenced unfinished as I turned to the mustang and stepped into the saddle.

I sadly watched as the small caravan disappeared in the distance of the valley.

CHAPTER 14

The town of Clear Fork lay asleep in the predawn hours as I sat watching from an overlooking, windswept hill. A temperate breeze softly touched my cheeks as it whispered past. Though the breeze was warm, I shuddered. I did not shudder from the cold on the outside; I shuddered from the cold that lay deep within. How, at this moment, I so longed to be in Santa Fe holding Rosa tightly in my arms. To be able to wake up and see the sparkle in her beautiful eyes and feel the warmth of her lips pressed to mine. To again hear her soft and comforting voice. But that was gone and … I was here.

All the months I had spent meticulously planning my return had not even remotely prepared me for the cold, empty feeling that rode beside me like a faceless angel of death. It was then I realized a man could never really make ready for his own chosen death. I felt scared and very much alone. With reservation, I bumped my heels against the ribs of my horse as I rode into town under the cover of darkness.

Panic continued to tighten its icy fingers around me to the point I felt like turning my horse and spurring away, never looking back. Then I thought of Tig. The sight of him staggering toward me after a murderous bullet tore into his back, and asking for my help when I could do nothing, played over and over in my mind in painful detail. The memory of holding him in my arms as he struggled for his last breath brought back the deep-rooted bitterness and hatred that had eaten away at me for such a long time. I clinched my jaws as I reined the mustang down a back alley.

In the remote New Mexico town of Clear Fork, J.B. Ross and his son Bert were the big fish in the big pond. And the big pond just so happened to be the sprawling Box-T ranch, which they managed. Resting assured I would not receive a fair trial in such circumstance, I had made my plans accordingly.

Pulling my horse to a halt behind the limestone-blocked courthouse, I dismounted. Trying the knob on the back door, I found it locked. With my pocketknife, I quietly jimmied the lock until the latch relented and I quickly stepped inside. Walking into the dark, empty courthouse, I struck a match and cupped it in my hands. A chill went up my spine as I stood in the hallowed halls. It was a place where justice was sworn to be upheld and served, even for the poor and the downtrodden. However, I knew in this case it was a place where the truth would be distorted and even fabricated to protect the rich, the powerful, and the guilty. But it really made no difference, for I would exact my own justice right here in this very building.

Walking over to the witness stand, I reached out and felt the smooth wood railing beneath my fingers before I sat down in the rigid armchair. Allowing the match to burn out, my eyes gradually grew accustom to the weak light that filtered in from the uncurtained windows. From the witness chair, I sat staring out at the bare, empty benches. One day soon, I knew the same benches that now sat peaceful and quiet would be filled with people clamoring for my hanging.

Standing, I picked up the chair and turned it upside down. Beneath the hard wooden seat were two twisted wires crisscrossing underneath, forming the pattern of an x and holding the frame and the legs taut. Taking a thin piece of string from my shirt pocket, I tied one end to one of the wires. Pulling my pistol from its holster, I ran the string through the trigger guard before pulling it tight underneath the wooden seat and tying it off. The pistol was held out of sight above the binding wires. Turning the chair back over, I sat down. With only a slight bend of my upper body my hand could reach the butt of the forty-five. Closing my fingers around the walnut grip of the gun, I pulled. The small string snapped easily as the gun filled my hand. Standing, I carefully checked the pistol before once again securing it underneath the chair.

For several minutes I stood facing the empty benches. "J.B. Ross, the day of reckoning is drawing near for you and your son. May both of your thievin', murderin' souls rot in hell."

Quietly stepping into the dark, I closed the courthouse door behind me. Removing my gun belt, I placed it in my saddlebags. As I did so, I retrieved my small black diary and tucked it safely into my coat pocket. Picking up the reins, I led my horse quietly through the silent shadows of the alley.

Tying the horse to the hitch rail in front of the sheriff's office, I stepped up on the boardwalk. The weathered gray boards rang hollow underneath the heels of my boots. Taking a deep breath, I reached out and placed my hand on the doorknob. I knew once I turned that knob there could be no turning back. This would be my final, fate-sealing step. I momentarily hesitated. Taking a deep breath, I opened the door and stepped inside.

A lantern, hanging from a metal bracket on the wall, bathed the office in a yellowish light. The sheriff, whom I had never met, looked up from his desk. He was an elderly man, more so than I would have figured him to be. He sat bareheaded, his gray hair disheveled, as he had not yet prepared himself for the upcoming day. The morning's first cup of coffee sat steaming in front of him alongside an orderly stack of wanted dodgers. I could tell by the look on his face, as his eyes prudently studied me, he did not know who I was.

"Can I help you, son?" he asked as he leaned over and picked up the coffee cup in front of him.

I nodded as I sat down in a chair in front of his desk. "Yes, sir," I replied. "I reckon you can. My name is Chance Tucker."

The expression on his face quickly changed as the cup rested against his lips, the contents untouched. His eyes shot a quick, longing glance toward his gun belt that hung on a peg out of his reach.

I smiled as our eyes met. "That's not necessary," I said as I placed my Winchester on the desk in front of him. "I came to turn myself in."

I could tell he was taken aback and did not know how to respond. Therefore, he just sat there staring at me, still holding the cup to his lips. I am sure everything he had heard about me was that I was a cattle rustler and a cold, ruthless killer, how I had cold-bloodedly murdered three innocent men of the Box-T when they came upon my partner and me as we were pushing stolen stock. I judged from his reaction that he was somehow expecting me to look like some kind of bloodthirsty wolf.

Slowly, he lowered the cup back to the scarred surface of the desk. "Okay ... okay," he finally stammered. "Okay, we can do that," he said as he cautiously rose from his chair. As he again eyed my Winchester, he motioned toward his gun. "I need to get my pistol."

I nodded. "I don't have any more guns on me, Sheriff. I've never killed an innocent man in my life and I'm sure not gonna start now."

Reaching over, he pulled his pistol from the hanging holster. As he stepped from around the desk, I stood up.

"I reckon I need to search ya' anyway."

I raised my hands to shoulder height and slowly turned around. He quickly patted me down. "Step through here," he said as he reached around me and opened a wooden door.

The door led to a narrow hallway that housed two cells on each side. All four of the cells sat vacant. With the building being made of brick, coupled with the steel bars of the cells, the jail had a cold and ominous feel about it.

"It's been pretty quiet around here as of late, so I reckon you can have your pick."

I stepped into the first cell I came to. As I stood staring at the small cot, I heard the barred door clang shut behind me. The sound made me wince.

"Chance Tucker, you say?"

I slowly turned around and faced the sheriff through the steel bars. "Yes, sir. Chance Tucker."

The sheriff reached up and scratched his head. "I reckon you're not exactly what I was expecting."

"I imagine not," I replied.

As the sheriff turned and went back through the door, I walked over to the cot. Staring up at the small east-facing window, I watched as the darkness slowly faded, giving way to the light of a new day. With the morning sun shining through the barred window, I saw the side of a two-story, redbrick building across the narrow alley from my cell. Stepping up on the edge of the cot, I peered over the bottom ledge of the window. Painted in faded letters on the side of the building were the words *Clear Fork Bank & Trust*. Sitting back down, I stared at the steel bars that surrounded me.

Within minutes, the sheriff came back through the door holding a cup of coffee in his hand. This time his hair was freshly combed, his shirt tucked neatly in his pants. "I brought you a cup of coffee," he said as he held out the cup. "I don't have nothin' to doctor it up with, so I hope you take it black."

I rose from the cot. Taking the tin cup through the steel bars, I nodded. "Thanks. I appreciate it."

"Well, ya' might want to try it before ya' thank me, I made it myself. I never was much of a cook, even when it comes to coffee. My wife, Emma, God rest her soul, used to say I was the only person that she knew that could scorch water to the point it was undrinkable." I smiled at the comment.

"I reckon I was a little caught off guard when you came in this morning and I don't guess I properly introduced myself. I'm the sheriff here in Clear Fork, my name's William Brady."

"It's nice to meet ya' Sheriff," I replied as I stuck my right hand out through the bars. "But I wish it was under different circumstances."

The sheriff cautiously looked at my hand a

moment before he accepted it. He chuckled at his action. "I reckon I'm a little bamboozled by this whole situation. In my thirty-five years of sheriffin', I can't remember ever having someone that's wanted for rustlin' and murder come turn themselves in like you done. Naw," he said shaking his head, "usually the only way they surrender is if they're leakin' blood in a goodly amount or if they just plum run out of bullets to shoot at me with."

"I reckon that's true," I replied as I took a sip from the cup. I agreed with the sheriff on his coffee making. I figured if I accidentally spilled some on the steel bars, there was a strong possibility it would eat right through them. "I reckon if I was a rustler and a murderer, I wouldn't have turned myself in, either."

My statement put a perplexed look on the sheriff's face. "Son, I'll be honest with ya'," he said as he slowly shook his head, "I don't rightly know if you're guilty or innocent, it's not my job, but J.B. Ross is a pretty big man in this part of the country. If it weren't for the Box-T and a couple of the smaller spreads around here, this town probably wouldn't survive. I reckon in some way, whether the people of Clear Fork particularly like him or not, they feel beholden to him for their survival, as well. The killin' of three of his men has some of the town folks in an uproar and there's some of 'em that's gonna want to stretch your neck soon as they find out you're here."

"I figgered as much, Sheriff. When I came to

turn myself in, I knew I was drawin' a hand in a rigged game."

The sheriff wrinkled his brow, his eyes studying me before he turned and headed toward the door.

"Sheriff," I called out. "Do you feel beholden to Ross like some of the others you mentioned?"

I saw his body stiffen at the meaning of my words. When he turned, his eyes held a fire. "Let me tell ya' somethin' son, the only thing I'm beholden to is this star I'm wearing on my chest," he said as he pointed an arthritic finger toward his badge. "Me, nor this badge, can be run roughshod over, nor can either of us be bought. I've worn this badge for over thirty years and it has always been that way. It'll be that way 'til they either take it away from me or they pat down a shovel full of dirt over my face."

Our eyes held before I felt a smile crease the corner of my mouth. "I figgered that also."

"I will give you a little advice though," he said. "You need to get yourself a lawyer."

"I don't reckon there's much need in that," I replied. "What little money I have would do more good on my folks' farm than it would paddin' some lawyer's pocket. It might make a little difference back home. It ain't gonna make one bit of difference here."

After the sheriff left, I sat down on the cot and opened my diary. I thumbed through the worn, yellowing pages until I came to one that was blank. Picking up the stubby pencil, I began writing. Outside, the town slowly came alive. I heard the clomping of hooves and the rattling of trace chains as a wagon lumbered its way down the narrow street. I could hear laughter as two cowboys trotted past, their spurs jingling in time with their horse's movements. Everyone seemed to be going about their lives as normal. I figured they were probably as guilty as the rest of us of not fully appreciating the freedom we took for granted each day until it was suddenly gone.

After filling several pages, I found myself idly holding the pencil between my fingers as my thoughts drifted back to my folks' farm in Tennessee. It had been well over a year since I had last written them a letter. And it had been even longer since I had been in the same place long enough to receive a letter from them as well. As much as I missed them, I was very glad they were a long ways away from me now.

I caught myself thinking of Rosa and Diego, wondering how things were going for them as they built their new life in Santa Fe. I suppose we all have regrets in our lives, but the one regret I have, which I concede is a selfish one, is never knowing what true happiness with the right woman could be. The reality was knowing that when I finally did find that one special woman, it was too late, my life had already been determined. I succumbed to the fact, long ago, that I would never know the feeling of lying in the arms of the only woman I have ever loved. Even though I knew I couldn't, I deeply regret never telling Rosa that I loved her. I guess if it was of any consolation to her, which I suppose it really wasn't, I knew she was aware of my feelings, anyway.

Later that same morning, Sheriff Brady came walking through the door with two men following close behind. Both of the men were wearing highly polished deputy badges. It only took a quick glance at their wide eyes and their overly cautious movements to realize neither of them were seasoned lawmen.

The sheriff spoke, "Chance, these men are my newly sworn deputies." I could tell by the concerned look on his face and the lack of enthusiasm in his voice, even though he made a valiant effort to mask it, that he felt no more security in the men than I did. I supposed in a small town sometimes there were not many options on such a short notice. "They're gonna help ensure your safety while you're in my custody. By this afternoon, I'll probably know when your trial will be held. I figger, for everyone's sake, the sooner the better."

I nodded as I glanced at the two deputies. The shotguns they awkwardly held in their hands seemed to be as out of place as a ballroom gown on a backwoods country girl. I had no doubt if I was going to make trial it would have to be sooner rather than later to even have a chance of making an appearance in the courtroom.

"This is Deputy Sorenson and Deputy Finch," the sheriff said.

I pegged Sorenson, with his slight build and

soft hands, to be some type of merchant. His small eyes fidgeted nervously on his narrow face. With Finch, I couldn't tell for sure but with the flakes of hay clinging to his clothes and the aroma of his boots, I figured him to be a hostler at the livery stable.

I started to put my hand through the bars but I was reluctant, fearing that as nervous as the two men appeared to be, they might very well shoot somebody. And who that unfortunate one might be was anybody's guess.

The sheriff motioned the two deputies from the room. "Two of us will be here at all times. If you need anything just give me or my men a holler. We'll accommodate you if we can."

"Your deputies seem like good men. I don't want to see 'em get hurt on my account."

Brady nodded as deep concern shadowed his face. "Me either," he said solemnly. "Me either."

By early afternoon, the word of me being in jail spread through the desert town like a fire through a dry cane field. Soon afterward, the first discontented rumblings began echoing up and down the dusty street.

As night drew its dark blanket over the town, the rumblings outside the jail grew in intensity as the number of men gathering in the street continued to swell. I had the unsettling feeling the town of Clear Fork was about to be torn apart at the seams.

CHAPTER 15

I was jarred awake from a light sleep by the shout of a man's voice. "Sheriff! Send that killer out here!"

I quickly got to my feet. I could see the glow of torches from the street as the shadows they cast danced threateningly through the small window above my head. I could tell from the loud grumblings that followed close behind the man's words, the mob was large and was probably primed with a misdirected, whiskey-fueled hatred. My heart was thumping against my chest as I gripped the steel bars that held me caged and defenseless.

"If ya' don't send him out we're gonna come get him! There ain't nobody gonna murder three Box-T cowboys and not swing for it!" A chorus of shouts reverberated through the crowd.

"You men go home!" The sheriff hollered back. "There ain't gonna be no lynching here tonight! He's gonna get a fair trial like anybody else that's a prisoner of mine!"

The wooden door that separated the sheriff's office from the cells suddenly opened and the deputy named Sorenson quickly stepped inside. After shutting the door behind him, I heard a padlock click into place on the other side. The jail was dark other than the faint light of the torches that spilled through the window and reflected on the deputy's distraught face. His narrow eyes darted toward me before nervously turning to stare at the door that was potentially the last line of defense from the angry mob. I could see the whites of his knuckles as he anxiously clutched the shotgun in his hands.

"How many are out there?" I asked.

"I don't know for sure," he panted. "But there's a bunch. A whole damn bunch."

As I stood listening to the tumultuous shouts of the frenzied mob, the deputy volunteered, "The Ross's have been over at the saloon all evening buying drinks for half the town and stirring the pot something fierce. I don't imagine all the men out there necessarily agree with vigilante-style justice, I figure most are just too scared of the Ross's to stand up to them. J.B. Ross has run this part of the country for a pretty long time and he can ruin any man that he so chooses. I've seen him do it before. More than once."

Even though I could tell the deputy was scared, and justifiably so, he gave no indication of backing down from the ominous threat outside.

"Deputy, what do you do for a living?"

"I own the hardware store."

"So what are you doing this for? Aren't you afraid of Ross ruining you?"

In the dim light, I could see his shoulders slowly sink before he spoke. "He already has. He ruined me years ago, just like he ruined a lot of people in this town."

"What do ya' mean?"

Sorenson relaxed his grip on the shotgun as he turned and faced me. I could see the agony in his eyes and I could hear the shame in his voice when he spoke. "Ross and some of his cowboys ran roughshod over the people of this town until we cowered in front of him like a beat-down dog. He took away the one thing that makes a man, the only thing a man ever really owns ... he took away our pride."

"Why didn't the Sheriff do anything to stop it?"

"Oh, he tried to," he said as he despondently shook his head. "But the people of Clear Fork were all so scared of Ross and his men, including me, that nobody would testify against him. There was nothing Sheriff Brady could do. This morning when the sheriff came and asked for my help I knew it would be dangerous and I said no, like all of the others had. However, after he left, I got to thinking about it and I just couldn't live that way anymore. I made a decision right then and there that I had rather die standing up like a man than to go on living with my tail tucked between my legs."

He paused as he took a deep breath. "You probably don't know what it's like to look at yourself in a mirror and see nothing but shame ... I do."

The next voice I heard sent a fire through me like a hot branding iron touching bare hide. "Sheriff!" J.B. Ross hollered out. "You've got five minutes to send that killer out here before we bust in there and take him! You might as well save yourself some grief and possibly the lives of them two so-called deputies you got in there with you! Their blood's gonna be on your hands, not mine! All we want is Chance Tucker. Send him out here!"

I knew what Ross said was not true. The blood of the two deputies as well as the blood of the sheriff, if it came to that, would all be on my hands if it were on anyone's. As I watched Sorenson, I saw his fingers again tighten on the shotgun. "Deputy, tell the sheriff I need to talk to him."

Sorenson turned and looked questioningly at me before he knocked on the locked door. "Sheriff, the prisoner wants to talk to you."

I heard the lock being removed before the door opened and the sheriff stepped into the hallway. "Sorenson, wait in the other room," he said. "Keep your head down and stay away from the windows." The deputy nodded before pulling the door shut. "What is it, Chance?"

The lines in Brady's drawn face seemed deeper and more distinct than they had been earlier in the day.

His eyes sagged with undeniable worry. "Sheriff, when I turned myself in to you, I knew my life was over, I was as good as dead. I can accept that. But I can't accept being responsible for the death of you and your deputies. That's not how it was supposed to be."

The sheriff studied me through searching eyes before he spoke. "I haven't quite figured out why you did turn yourself in. When I heard about the killings out at Hell's Gate and I heard who the three men were, I'll be honest with ya', I was glad they were dead. So were a lot of people around here, even though they wouldn't dare say so aloud. Those three were some of the sorriest excuses for men that the Almighty has ever put on the face of the earth. I figured they got exactly what they deserved. But something that's been puzzling me is when I went out there and got to looking around I found the body of a young man down in the bottom of a gully. It looked like someone had tried to bury him by caving the bank in on top of him. It wasn't quite deep enough, though, and the coyotes got to him." He paused as he continued studying me. "There was enough left of him that I could tell he had been shot in the back."

My head slowly dropped to my chest as I clinched my eyes tightly shut, trying to rid the graphic picture that flooded my mind. The thought of Tig's body being ripped and torn by coyotes sent a wave of sickness through my body. "His name was Tig Jones," I stammered as my fingers gripped the coldness of the steel bars. "He was my partner and my best friend. Them son of a bitches murdered him in cold blood the same way they tried to murder me. It was the Ross's that ordered it. It was the Ross's that were stealing the syndicate's cattle."

I could see the sheriff carefully weighing my words. "So, tell me Chance, why did you turn yourself in?"

The sickness that I felt passed as it was replaced with the bitter taste of hate. I shook my head. "I can't tell ya' why, sheriff," I said as I looked him in the eye. "But I've got my reasons."

He grumbled at my answer. "Well, I ain't got a clue what's on your mind. But whatever it is it ain't gonna work."

"Dammit, Sheriff, send me out there. Let them kill me. That's what's gonna happen, anyway. Don't make me responsible for ya'lls killings."

"I can't do that. I already tried to get Finch and Sorenson to leave, but they refused. I guess, whether any of us likes it or not, we're all sort of down this badger hole together. None of us can escape this ordeal no more than any of us can escape our own shadow." The sheriff paused as his weathered hand smoothed his gray mustache. "This thing is a little bigger than all of us, Chance. I think, in one way or another, everyone here is somehow fighting their own past. Perhaps, trying to someway dull the memory of distant regrets. Or, possibly, trying to somehow right some wrongs."

I weighed the sheriff's words carefully. Maybe he was right. Deep down I had always held myself responsible for Tig's death. If only I hadn't made the decision to follow those stolen cattle into Hell's Gate it would have been different. Tig would still be here and we would still be partners. Just two friends out riding the lonely country together, dreaming our dreams. It would be like old times. Sorenson had already told me about the demon that rode him. Maybe Finch fought that same battle.

"So tell me, Sheriff," I asked as I walked to the front of the cell and gripped the steel bars, "What regret are you fightin'?"

I could see a pain slowly cloud his aging eyes, much like the fog rolling in off a secluded bay. He shook his head, but the question went unanswered.

As he headed toward the door, he stopped and turned around. "I got a wire in this afternoon. The circuit judge will arrive on the stage Monday morning. Your trial will be held the following day."

"You're optimistic, ain't ya'?"

He shrugged his shoulders. "What else do we have on our side?"

The shouts continued to pour in from the street as Sorenson stepped inside and closed the wooden door. I heard the voice of Brady as he once again called out to the crowd to clear the streets.

The deputy walked over to the front of the cell. He stood there a moment as if calculating his words.

"You aren't guilty, are you?"

I had run that same question through my mind a thousand times over the past three or four months. "I guess it depends how ya' look at it," I said. "According to most lawyers and judges nowadays, I suppose I probably am guilty. Not guilty of steeling cattle, but I'm guilty as hell of killin' them three men at Hell's Gate."

"Why did you kill them?"

"Because they murdered my best friend."

The deputy shook his head. "I suppose that's the difference between men like you and people like me. Men like yourself are willing to stand up for what's right and do something about it. Men like me see what needs to be done, we just don't seem to have the guts to do it. We sit back and wait for others, like you, to do it for us."

"Well, I suppose it's just like you said earlier, we all have to be able to look ourselves in the mirror."

The deputy nodded. "Looking back on it, do you wish you would have done things different?"

"You can't undo what's already done," I said. "But I reckon I would have done one thing different"

"What would that be?"

"I would've killed J.B. and Bert Ross before I turned myself in."

I saw the deputy's eyes stray from my face toward the barred window above my head. Instantly I turned. Searching through the darkness, my eyes caught the silhouette of a gunman atop the roof of the bank building across the alley.

"Duck!" I yelled.

As I dove to the floor, I heard the thundering boom of a rifle.

Quickly looking to Sorenson, I saw him stagger back into the steel bars of the adjacent cell as his shotgun slipped from his fingers and clattered to the floor. In the dim light, I could see the shock on his distorted face as he clutched at his left shoulder. A patch of his white shirt slowly turned crimson as blood seeped between his fingers. His eyes grew wide before his face paled and he slowly sank to the floor.

As the sheriff and Finch barged through the door, I hurriedly glanced up through the window. The man on the rooftop was in a kneeling position and poised for another shot. "On top of the bank!" I hollered.

The sheriff hastily raised his rifle to his shoulder. Before he could squeeze the trigger, a gunshot echoed from the street. As we watched through the window, the man on the rooftop slowly teetered back and forth before his limp body spilled from atop the building. With the close proximity of the bank and the jail, we heard bones snap like dried mesquite limbs as his body slammed into the hard-packed surface of the ground.

From out front of the jail a voiced called out. "You men get off of this street now! In ten seconds I start killing any man left standing here!"

I could hear an inaudible rumbling of voices before the man spoke again. "That includes you, Ross. If you don't get your men out of here, you're going to be the first one I cut in half with this scattergun."

"You may know my name, stranger," Ross growled. "But evidently you must not know who I am. I run this part of the country and anyone that bucks me ends up holding the short end of the stick. Usually the dead end!"

Sorenson was moaning as Sheriff Brady knelt by his side. Finch ran back to the front door of the office. With the door between the cells and the office open, I saw Finch cautiously peer around the edge of the window curtain.

I could hear a mumbling of voices in the alley as the body of the dead man was being removed. The noise from the street slowly died off before becoming eerily quiet. "How is he, Sheriff?" I asked as I peered down at Sorenson between the steel bars.

"He took a hard hit to his shoulder. But I think he'll make it if we get him to the doc."

"Sheriff," Finch called out, "someone's coming to the door."

Brady reached into his pocket and retrieved a handkerchief. "Hold this tight to that wound," he said as he grabbed his rifle. "We'll get you taken care of directly."

I heard a light knock on the office door before Brady pulled the door adjoining the cells closed behind him. The deep voice of the unknown man was low, but had a familiar sound to it. Try as I might, I could not put a face with the voice.

"How are you doing, Sorenson?" I asked

"I'm hurting like hell," he responded. I could see his face locked in a grimace. "Sheriff Brady seems to think I'm going to make it, but the way I feel I beg to differ."

"Hang in there. They'll get you fixed up shortly."

Within seconds, the sheriff came back through the door. "Come on, deputy," he said as he leaned down and helped Sorenson to his feet. "Let's get you over to the doc's before you make a mess of the whole floor."

"That's mighty considerate of you, Sheriff," the deputy grimaced. With his good arm draped over Brady's shoulder, they made their way through the hallway and out the front door.

"Hey, Finch, are you in there?" I called from my cell.

The deputy cracked the door open enough to stick his head through. "Yeah, I'm here. What do you want?"

"Who was the man outside earlier?"

He paused before he answered. "There were two of 'em," he said. "But I ain't at liberty to say."

"Why ain't ya'?"

"Cause I was told not to," he said, glancing over his shoulder as if afraid someone could possibly be in hearing distance. "The man that said to keep quiet was sort of a serious-lookin' type and the other looked like he could tear me plum into with his bare hands and not even break a sweat."

With that, he shut the door. After a cautious study out the window, I walked over and sat down on the cot.

Who could the men be and why were they here? Unless I read the sheriff wrong, and I don't think I did, he was as surprised as anyone. I guess it didn't really matter who they were. Without a doubt, they just saved four lives. One of those lives, temporarily, being mine.

It was close to an hour before I heard Brady return to his office. Shortly afterwards he opened the door between the office and cells. The light from the coal-oil lantern in the office illuminated the corridor between the cells.

I stood up as he approached. "How's your deputy, Sheriff?"

He drew in a deep breath before he spoke. "He was lucky. The doc said the bullet missed the bones. Other than being sore as Ol' Billy Thunder, he'll be fine."

A wave of relief swept over me. "I'm glad to hear that, Sheriff."

Brady nodded his agreement. I could tell something was deeply troubling him as he stood before me. "Son," he said. "I reckon you already know this as well as I do. You're not going to get a fair trial here. Don't get me wrong, there are some good decent folks here about, but with Ross staring over their shoulders they just aren't gonna risk their family's well-being to save you."

I could tell from the despondent look on his face as he wrinkled his brow he was taking the preconceived outcome personally. "Sheriff, it's like I told you earlier, I didn't come here expecting a fair trial."

He slowly nodded before his troubled eyes glanced down to his chest. Reaching up with his hand, his fingers traced the outline of the worn but polished badge that was pinned to the front of his shirt. "It seems ironic that the very same piece of metal that has given a man his life can be the very same thing that somehow rips the heart right out of him."

"I suppose that's just how life is sometimes, Sheriff," I nodded. "I suppose that's just how it is."

CHAPTER 16

The day of the trial seemed to arrive with the same swiftness as that of a blinking of an eye. The minutes seemed to have ticked by so slowly, yet somehow the days passed quickly. People continued to pour into the town of Clear Fork with an undeniable anticipation of the trial to come. I suppose, in reality, it was not just the anticipation of the trial itself that drew the people from miles around, but more so the expectancy of the hanging that was sure to follow.

It was mid-morning when the sheriff and the two deputies came to my cell. The sheriff's face was stoic but the deputies, not hardened to the tasks of a lawman, wore a grim look that tugged hard at their features.

As the sheriff unlocked the cell, he said, "Chance, I'm going to have to put these shackles on you. I know in your case it's not really necessary, but it's protocol."

I nodded as I stepped from the cell and held my hands in front of me. Brady clicked a set of handcuffs on my wrist before securing steel shackles around my ankles. Afterwards, he connected the two with a single chain.

Looking over at Sorenson and seeing the deputy's arm tightly bound in a sling, I asked, "How's that shoulder treatin' ya' deputy?"

"I suppose as good as could be expected," he replied. "Other than being sore, it's a little inconvenient when it comes to taking care of necessary business. If you know what I mean?"

I smiled at the comment. "I reckon that's one of the downsides of being a bachelor."

The deputy grinned.

The sheriff led me from the narrow corridor that housed the cells. The short chain of the shackles that bound my ankles forced me to shuffle my feet along the wooden floor. Momentarily halting in the office, all three men grabbed shotguns. After checking to make sure the shotguns, as well as the pistols they wore on their hips, were fully loaded, the sheriff said, "Well, men, are you ready?" Both deputies nodded in silence. "Let's get this done then."

Sheriff Brady opened the door and stepped out on the boardwalk before halting, his eyes warily studying the surroundings. I heard both hammers of his shotgun click as he locked them back in a cocked position. He turned and nodded to me and I shuffled through the door behind him. I was not prepared for what I saw. The street was packed with people standing shoulder –to –shoulder; men, women and even children all staring at me. As I uncomfortably scanned the crowd, the contempt on most faces and the disgust in their eyes was obvious. The sight caused my throat to go tight. As I shuffled along behind the sheriff, one deputy on each side of me, I stared straight ahead, trying not to see the disturbing look in the people's faces. The chains that bound me rattled and clanked with my awkward movement.

The walk from the jail to the courthouse was no more than a couple of blocks, but as I shuffled along time seemed to stand still. The large crowd before us apprehensively parted, making just enough room for us to go by before melting together again as soon as we passed. At first, the talk of the crowd had been low and among themselves, but the closer we got to the stone courthouse, the talk became angry shouts directed toward me.

"You're wasting a lot of time, Sheriff. Hang him now!" A man hollered from somewhere back in the crowd.

Another man yelled out, "We'll see how tough you are dancing at the end of a rope! You spineless coward!"

There was a woman standing in close proximity of the courthouse door when we neared. Next to her side was a young boy of maybe ten years of age.

"Do you see this man, son?" I heard the woman ask the small boy as she leaned down next to his ear. "This is what happens to sinners who break the commandments of the Lord. He reaches down and smites them before sending them to burn in Hell."

Out of the corner of my eye, I saw the boy nod his head. "But what if he ain't guilty?" the boy asked.

As I followed the sheriff through the doorway, I heard the woman admonish the child. "Don't be silly. He's guilty and he will be hanged."

The courthouse was packed full with spectators, all of whom fell silent as I walked into the room. The throng of people from the outside funneled in behind us as they clamored for the limited amount of standing room against the back wall. The sheriff led me down the narrow center aisle between the rows of crowded benches before stopping near the front at what I figured to be the defendant's table. There the sheriff removed the cuffs and shackles from my wrists and ankles before we both sat down.

Deputy Finch immediately moved to the wall nearest where we sat. Deputy Sorenson walked back to the doorway. After a tussle, he was finally able to move the people from the entryway enough to be able to close the courthouse door. The grumblings from the excluded crowd outside instantly followed. Sorenson put his back against the door, his shotgun held ready in front of him as he stared straight ahead.

Glancing over at the table next to where we sat,

I saw two men who I assumed to be prosecuting attorneys for the state. Seated next to them were J.B Ross and his son Bert. The elder Ross stared across the aisle at me. When our eyes met, he smiled. It was not only a smile of arrogance and pure evil; it was much more than that. It was a smile of confidence at the victory that was sure to prevail by the bastardizing of justice.

As I looked away I said to myself, "You'd better enjoy that smile, you son of a bitch, because you won't be smiling when I put a bullet hole right between your eyes."

We had been seated for mere minutes when twelve jurors filed in, each taking their places in the jury box. A short while later the door to the judge's chambered opened and the bailiff entered. "All rise," he stated. "The honorable Judge Vickers presiding."

The elderly judge walked into the courtroom. His black robe rustled with his movement as he made his way to the bench before sitting down.

Peering down at the paperwork in front of him, he waved his hand without looking up. "Be seated," he said as he reached into his robe and produced a pair of reading spectacles.

After reading the paperwork, he looked out over the courtroom. "Will the defendant please stand up. Today we are hearing the case of the State of New Mexico versus Chance Tucker. The charges against the defendant include the theft of three hundred and twenty seven head of cattle from the Box-T ranch as well as the murder of three men who were gainfully employed by the ranch aforementioned." Tilting his head forward to peer over his glasses at me, he asked, "How do you plead to these charges, Mister Tucker?"

"Innocent, your honor," I stated.

The judge wrinkled his brow, causing his bushy gray eyebrows to momentarily blend together as he continued looking at me. After a long pause he said, "Mister Tucker, I fail to see your counsel. Do you not have counsel present?"

"No, sir," I replied.

"Do you wish to have counsel present?"

"No, sir. I don't reckon I have much need for one."

"Then you choose to represent yourself?"

"Yes, sir."

The judge shook his head as he leaned back into his heavily padded chair. "As you wish, Mister Tucker. The state's prosecution may proceed when ready."

As the lead prosecutor for the state began delivering his opening statement, I looked over at the jury. The majority of the twelve-member jury appeared to be ranchers or cowboys, by their appearances. There were two or three I thought might possibly be local businessmen of one sort or the other.

Occasionally, the jurors would glance over at me as the prosecutor continued to lay out his case. Mostly their expressions were that of complete disdain.

Sheriff Brady leaned over to me. "The majority

of these jurors are friends of Ross," he whispered. "But there are two of them that own businesses here locally. One owns the livery stable, which relies heavily on the Box-T. The other is the teacher at the schoolhouse … the schoolhouse that Ross paid to have built."

I nodded my head as I watched the stacked deck being expertly played against me, one card at a time. It was not as if I expected anything else. If the truth were to come out, J.B Ross and his son would lose everything they had so unscrupulously built over the past twelve years. The theft of the syndicate's cattle and the murders committed to protect their dirty little secret would all be for naught. I knew Ross would not risk losing a fair fight when he could rig the game and guarantee victory. The stakes were simply too high.

As I studied the jury more, it was suddenly obvious who the two business owners were. They were the ones who surreptitiously bore the pained look on their faces. It was an unmistakable look. It was the look of men tied to a whipping post and being beat into submission. I knew J.B. Ross was the man wielding that cracking bullwhip.

" … and in the end," the prosecutor summarized, "we will show beyond any reasonable doubt that the man sitting before us, Chance Tucker, is not only guilty of steeling three hundred and twenty seven head of cattle from the reputable Box-T ranch, but is the malicious, cold-blooded killer of three honest hardworking men, as well." A large number of the gallery loudly voiced their approval as though they were ahmening a preacher's sermon.

The judge quickly slammed his gavel on the wooden surface of the bench. "That's enough of that," he warned as he sternly gazed over the rims of his glasses. "One more outburst like that and I will clear this courtroom. Is that understood?"

With the courtroom again silent, the judge looked to me. "Mister Tucker, would you like to give an opening statement?"

"No, sir, your honor. I reckon I don't see much need in it."

The judge again shook his head as he took a deep breath and leaned back in his chair. "Very well then," he sighed. "Counsel, you may call your first witness for the state."

"Thank you, your honor," the attorney said. "At this time I would like to call J.B. Ross to the stand."

J.B. Ross, with a sideways smirk on his face, confidently made his way to the witness stand. After being sworn in, he took a seat.

"Mister Ross, what is your capacity at the Box-T ranch?"

"I manage the Box-T. Not only do I manage the ranch, I oversee the entire operation and have for over twelve years."

"And if you would, Mister Ross, tell this court how you came to know this man sitting before us, Chance Tucker."

"Well, I reckon it was close to six months ago when him and another down-and-out fellow by the name of Steg or Stug, or … "

I felt anger slice through me like a knife blade as I sprang to my feet. "His name was Tig! Tig Jones!" I shouted. "You son of a bitch! You ought to at least know the name of the man you had killed!" I yelled as I sprang toward Ross.

Sheriff Brady immediately jumped to his feet and grabbed hold of me. Somewhere in the back of my mind, I could hear the judge repeatedly slamming his gavel and calling for order, but I did not care.

The judge's face went red as he continued pounding his gavel and calling for order. "Get this man out of my courtroom!" I heard him hollering.

Everything was in a state of total chaos as the sheriff and the two deputies converged on me. As they began dragging me toward the doorway through which the jurors had entered the courtroom, I continued cussing Ross until they had me out of the room and the door closed behind.

Through the closed door, I could hear the gavel continue to ring on the wooden surface of the bench, before the courtroom slowly succumbed to order.

I could feel my body still shaking with anger as Sheriff Brady stood in front of me with a firm grasp on my shoulders. "Chance! Calm down, dammit! Get a hold of yourself!"

I felt my body slowly begin to relax as I stood

in the midst of the sheriff and the two deputies.

"Holy Hell!" Sorensen mumbled. "I ain't ever seen anything quite like that! I thought you was gonna kill Ross right then and there."

"If it had been up to me," Deputy Finch spewed, "I'd of let him do it. Everybody knows we'd all be better off with that bastard dead."

"Shut up!" Sheriff Brady snapped. "Don't either of you ever let me hear you say something like that again! Never! You understand me! Never!"

I could tell by the fierce look in the sheriff's eyes that he had taken the deputy's word as insult to the badge that he wore on his chest. I knew it was the same badge that justified the reasons for which all his commitments and sacrifices, his entire life, had been made.

When everyone calmed down, I realized Finch had recognized the same as I had in the sheriff's reaction. "I'm sorry, Sheriff," the deputy said. "I didn't mean nothin' by it."

"Me either," Sorensen added, even though he had said nothing out of line.

I knew that I was the one responsible for the entire outbreak, but I had not calmed down enough to feel repentant about the ordeal. I was still anxiously awaiting the opportunity of putting a bullet between the eyes of J.B. Ross. The only way I would feel repentant about what happened is if I were not allowed back into the courtroom to sit on the chair in the witness stand, where my pistol was stashed.

As the four of us stood in silence, the judge entered the room. After raking us with his stern gaze, he said, "Sheriff, I want this man in cuffs and shackles at all times. He will not be allowed into my courtroom until the prosecution has pled their case. He then may present his case, if and only if, he observes the rules of the court. If he does not choose to conduct himself in such a manner, this trial will be over. He will be judged guilty, and will be hanged. Do you understand that, sheriff?"

"Yes, your honor," the sheriff responded.

"If you feel you are not capable of controlling your prisoner, I will arrange to obtain the services of some men who are."

Sheriff Brady's jaws clinched tight before he spoke again. "That won't be necessary. It will not happen again."

The judge turned his hard gaze on me. "Did I make myself quite clear to *you*, Mister Tucker?" I nodded.

After Judge Vickers left the room, the sheriff once again began securing the restraints on my wrists and ankles. It was easy to tell the sheriff was still peeved at me for my outburst and the rebuking he suffered at the hands of the judge. When Brady tightly latched the cuffs on my wrists, they bit sharply into my skin.

No one spoke as we sat in the sequestered room. The only sound was an occasional squeaking of one of the wooden chairs. I could only guess at what the other men were thinking or feeling. As for myself, I felt only anxiousness. An anxiousness to finally get my hands on my pistol with J.B and Bert Ross staring down the barrel of the Colt forty-five.

CHAPTER 17

Time slowly ticked by as we continued to wait in the secluded room. The anger that had caused me to explode in the courtroom had vanished. Left in its place was the stark reality of the dire circumstance that encompassed me. I became edgy as the situation grated like a hoof rasp on my nerves. As I sat in silence, I noticed an occasional glance from the sheriff and the two deputies, but nothing was said.

I found myself mentally going through the steps, repeatedly, that I long ago had planned. I knew that when I pulled that pistol from under that chair and killed the Ross's, I too would be killed. Even from the earliest stages of my planning, I realized in order for me to get close enough to kill the men that were responsible for Tig's death, that is how it would have to be.

Would it be the sheriff who killed me? Or perhaps Finch or Sorensen, I wondered. Possibly, it would be one of the spectators who were crowded into the courtroom. After I thought about it more, I hoped it would be the latter. I preferred that neither the sheriff nor the deputies would be forced to live with that fact.

I felt my heartbeat quicken when the bailiff opened the door. I saw him glance at me to make sure I was shackled before he spoke. "The judge is ready for the prisoner, Sheriff."

The sheriff nodded as we all stood up.

"Sheriff, I would like to say something before we go in there."

"What is it, son?"

"I just wanted to say I appreciate the way that you and your deputies have treated me while I've been in your custody. I have a lot of respect for men like yourself. The only problem it seems is there's just not enough men cut from the same mold as you."

"I appreciate that," he said as he stood before me. "I treat any prisoner of mine that way."

I smiled. "I know. That's what I'm talking about."

My statement put a near smile on his face.

"Sorensen, Finch ... thanks," I said as I turned toward the door. "I'm ready, Sheriff."

The chains from my handcuffs and leg irons rattled loudly as I shuffled through the door behind the sheriff. The air in the courtroom was strained and stifled with hate. I could only imagine the distorted lies that had been told during my absence.

Finch and Sorensen took up the same positions around the room that they had occupied earlier. I stood at the defendant's table, Sheriff Brady at my side.

"Mister, Tucker," the judge said, "since you have chosen to represent yourself, by law, you may cross-examine any witness that has testified under oath before this court. Do you wish to do so?"

"No, sir."

"Then," he said, "would you like to take the stand in your own defense?"

"Yes, sir," I nodded. "I would."

"Very well then," he said as he waved his hand toward the witness stand. "This court is ready when you are."

As I shuffled toward the witness stand, I felt a sickening feeling growing in the pit of my stomach. Under the bailiff's instructions, I placed my left hand on the bible and raised my right hand as high as my restraints allowed, which was barely above my waist.

I did not hear a word the bailiff said as I stood before him. Nothing seemed real. It was as though I was in some sort of nightmare that, try as I might, I could not awaken myself from. Everything seemed fuzzy and indistinct. Suddenly, I was aware of the bailiff standing before me, expectantly staring.

As realization returned, it dawned on me that he was awaiting my response. "I do."

As the bailiff walked away, the judge said, "Be seated, Mister Tucker. You may begin when ready."

I sat down. With the familiar feel of the chair beneath me, everything seemed to suddenly come into a crystal-clear focus.

Taking a deep breath, I began, "About six months ago, me and my partner hired on with the Box-T. My partner's name was Tig Jones. Did you hear that, Ross? His name was Tig Jones!"

"Continue, Mister Tucker," the judge warned with a raised eyebrow.

J.B. Ross smirked as he leaned back in his chair and crossed his arms in front of him. Bert leaned over and whispered something into his father's ear. They both smiled.

As I again started telling my story, the front door of the courthouse opened. Everyone turned to see why my speaking came to a halt. From the glaring light of the bright sunshine, a man stepped into the doorway. He was a rather large man, his skin bronzed and weathered from the Texas sun. His eyes were a cool gray, matching the color of his drooping mustache. As I sat staring, John McCandle walked into the courtroom and put his back to the wall. Our eyes met. I found no feeling in his gray eyes. There was no feeling in mine. Between us there was no emotion expressed at all.

"Mister Tucker," the judge encouraged. "You may continue."

I nodded as my gaze slowly left that of John McCandle's. "Me and Tig noticed within weeks after we began working for the Box-T that the number of cattle on the east side of the range, where we rode, seemed to be dwindling.

"We reported our concerns about our tallies to Bert Ross as well as to J.B. The only thing we received for our efforts was a severe chewin' out. I became suspicious at that point. But I had no reason to believe, at that time, that J.B. and Bert Ross were actually stealing cattle from the very syndicate for which they worked."

The prosecuting attorney immediately leapt to his feet. "Objection, your honor!" he yelled. "I will not idly sit by and watch as this man not only attempts to discredit the honor and integrity of this court, but also makes slanderous statements directed toward one of the most upstanding citizens in this community."

"Objection overruled. The court will allow Mister Tucker to tell his side of the story. Continue, Mister Tucker."

The attorney grumbled as he returned to his chair.

"One afternoon we came across the tracks of ten or twelve tightly bunch cows that had been driven south toward Hell's Gate. We followed them across Alder Creek and all the way to a ravine that led directly down into the canyons. It was nearing sundown and neither my partner or myself was familiar with the rugged gorge so we decided to make camp for the night right west of there."

I could tell even though the crowd was still hostile, at least some of them were listening to my story.

I guess that is all I could hope for. I suppose it really did not matter. At least after I pulled my pistol and killed the Ross's, they would know my reasoning. Not really much consolation for a dead man, I suppose.

"The next morning we followed the cattle down the steep trail that led directly into the maze of canyons. We were about halfway down into the canyon when somebody opened fire on us. My horse was hit with the first volley, but she carried me all the way to the valley floor before she gave out on me. Tig barreled in right behind me as we took cover in a cluster of boulders.

"The best we could figure, there were four or possibly five men shootin' at us. They kept us pinned down 'til dark. We realized our only chance to escape was to sneak out under the cover of darkness, so we did. We walked all night long following the shallow stream to the west hoping it led the way out. It didn't."

I saw the prosecutor again stand up. "Your honor, with all due respect, does this court have to sit and listen to this man continue to tell such a wild yarn, when it is very obvious this man will lie all day long in an attempt to save his own skin? We have already heard *truthful* testimony from Mister Ross, as well from his son Bert Ross. The truth, without a doubt, contradicts what the defendant is saying. In actuality, the story we are being subjected to is the exact opposite of the truth. He is merely turning the truth upside down, your honor."

"The defendant will be allowed to tell his story,

counsel," the judge stated. "And, if I may say so, since you seem to be so concerned about the time, maybe you could limit your interruptions."

The attorney returned to his seat, obviously irritated. Slamming his notebook closed, he placed his glasses on top of his papers and leaned back in his chair.

"As the sun came up the following morning we found that the stream disappeared beneath the back wall of a box canyon. Knowing the stream was our only hope of getting out alive; we laid on our backs and crawled into the narrow tunnel. To our surprise, we found a small cavern inside the mountain. We started a fire and warmed up as much as we could. Soon after, we crawled through another tunnel that exited the cavern to the west."

The prosecuting attorney again came to his feet. "Your honor, again I must say, this court has already heard this story. The cattle thieves holed up in the cave and came out shooting in order to try to escape justice," the attorney said as he spread his arms wide. "Is this really necessary?"

I could tell the judge was losing patience. "Counsel, if you would like to remain in my court, you will, I reiterate, you will hold your objections until what I consider a proper time."

The attorney sat down and began talking to J.B. Ross.

"Tig was in front of me as we left the cave.

When he turned to tell me there was no one waiting for us outside, he was shot in the back." I paused as my jaws clinched tight. "He died in my arms late that afternoon."

I stopped a moment and closed my eyes as the pain of that horrendous memory came flooding back. When I again raised my head, I looked into the eyes of J.B. Ross. I never knew that hate could be as vehemently powerful as it was in me that very moment.

It took me a few moments before I regained my composure. "Shortly afterwards, I found my way out of the cave through an opening in the ceiling. Once outside, I smelled smoke and heard men's voices. I waited 'til dark and worked my way around toward the glow of the fire. The fire was built near the mouth of the cave. I knew the fire was built where it was to make sure me and Tig would never leave there alive. I snuck down closer to the fire and listened from the darkness.

"There were three men around that fire. I listened to them talk. What I heard the men talking about was that J.B. and Bert Ross had given them orders to kill us in order to protect the truth being known of how the Ross's were stealing the syndicates cattle."

"Objection!" the prosecutor shouted. The court room erupted.

The judge began banging his gavel. "Order! Order in this court!" He shouted. "I will have order!"

I could see by the look in some of the people's faces that the beliefs they had brought into the courthouse earlier in the day were wavering. When I looked at the jury, the same was not true. They left little doubt that their vote had been bought, paid for, and cast before they were ever seated in the courtroom.

"Objection again overruled," the judge stated before looking to me to continue.

"I came out of the darkness with a rifle in my hand. I killed two of the men quickly," I bluntly stated. "But not the other one, not the man named Dave. He was the one that murdered Tig. I shot him in the gut so he would die slow and painful just like my friend did."

The prosecutor was yelling above the roar in the room. "He admitted it, judge! He admitted he's a cold-blooded killer!"

It seemed like five minutes before the judge was able to bring somewhat of an order to the room. When the noise finally died away, he said, "Mister Tucker, is there anything else you would like to say?"

I could feel my heart racing wildly as I knew the long-awaited time had come. The festering vengeance and hatred that had for so long rotted and ripped and tore at my very soul now violently sought its release.

"No one gets away with murdering my best friend!" I yelled as I leaned down and reached underneath the chair for my forty-five. My fingers grasped for the walnut grip of the Colt.

It was not there! Frantically my fingers searched, but my pistol was not there.

I felt my heart sink as I slowly straightened in

the chair. I could feel everyone staring at me, not understanding. As I sat looking around the room, the eyes of John McCandle met mine. It was suddenly clear. He was the one. He was the one who found and removed the pistol I had hidden. His expression did not change, but I knew mine did. I had lost. In the most important battle of my life, I had been beaten. Now, not only would my life end, it would end in failure.

The jury returned to the courtroom after deliberating for less than a half hour.

"Foreman, has the jury reached a verdict?" the judge asked.

"Yes, your honor, we have," the man said. I sat staring forward. No thoughts. No feelings. "We the people find the defendant, Chance Tucker, *guilty* on all counts."

The Ross's, as well as the prosecuting attorneys, celebrated as did a handful of people in the courtroom. However, the majority sat silent.

"Chance Tucker, having been found guilty of the theft of three hundred and twenty seven head of cattle and the murder of three men, on the morning of April the twenty-second, at ten o'clock, you will be hanged by the neck until dead. May God rest your soul," the judge stated before slamming his gavel down one final time. "This court is adjourned."

I bowed my head as I sat amidst a storm of silence. "I'm sorry Tig," I mumbled. "I'm sorry."

CHAPTER 18

In my cell, I lay back on the small cot, waiting as the sand that measured time continued to slowly but steadily trickle away. With one day having gone by since my trial, twenty-four hours now became the gauge by which my life was measured.

Outside, I could hear the banging of a hammer and the grating of a saw as a gallows was being constructed for the purpose of my execution. Having witnessed a hanging once in the boomtown of Cripple Creek, Colorado, I knew dangling at the end of a rope was not a death I relished. Nevertheless, I had come to accept the fact that my life would end in such a manner.

Retrieving my diary, I began writing my final chapter. I found the writing of this last entry was the most difficult I had ever written. However, with resolve, I continued. The sunlight, which had earlier spilled through the barred window, had long faded into the recesses of the night as I closed my diary for the final time. Tying a string around the worn cover, I sat the small black book to my side.

I was sitting alone with my thoughts when the sheriff walked through the door. "Mind a little company?" he asked.

"No, not at all," I replied. "Actually, I'd welcome it."

"Good," he nodded as he brought a chair and sat it next to my cell. "I was sort of gettin' tired of arguing with myself. A fellar can only do that so long at one time without it plum drivin' him crazy."

I smiled at the comment. I could tell by the deep, troubled look etched on the sheriff's face that he seemed to have things on his mind, but there was an obvious reluctance to voice them. The ghostly shadows created by the flame of the coal-oil lantern in his office danced across our faces as we sat silent. Time continued to tick away.

When he finally spoke, his voice was distraught. "I just wanted you to know I'm turning in my badge. Tomorrow will be my last day."

I was caught off guard by his statement. "Why would you want to do somethin' like that, Sheriff?" I said as I shook my head. "This town needs you. Hell, it needs a whole lot more of men like you. Not fewer."

"My heart's just not in it anymore," he said as he looked to the tin star pinned on his chest. "After your trial, I've somehow lost faith in all the good that at one time this badge symbolized. You were railroaded. Everyone in this town, even if they didn't know it before your trial, they realize it now. Even Judge Vickers knows this court was a sham. Nevertheless, under his sworn oath to uphold his duty there was nothing he could do. The same was true for me. With this badge on my chest, there was nothing I could do to make things right. I had a chance at one time to have made things different. But I didn't." I could see the sheriff's jaws clinch in anger as he looked to the floor.

"Sheriff, I don't reckon I understand what you're saying. What more could you possibly have done to make things different?"

The sheriff sat staring down a long time before he slowly raised his head. "Do you remember when you asked what was it that drove me?"

"Yes, sir, I remember."

"Well, what's been driving me for a long time is knowing that J.B Ross and his son were not only rustlers, but in my heart I knew they were killers, as well. I knew. I couldn't prove it, but I knew."

"Sheriff, your deputy told me that you tried to do something about the Ross's, but no one would testify against them. They were all too scared of their own hide gettin' singed in the process. So, I don't see how you could've done anything more then you did."

"I could've killed Ross. I had J.B in my rifle sights six months ago. We were out in the desert, no one else around. But I didn't. I couldn't pull the trigger," he said as he ripped the badge from his chest. "It was this damn badge that kept me from doing what was right! It was this damn badge!"

I watched his knuckles whiten as he clutched the tin star in his hand and gazed forlornly upon it as though it was a curse. "Not only did my lack of action cost your friend his life, now it has cost you your life as well. It's my fault … I'm sorry, son."

I sat on the edge of the cot as I tried to make sense of what the sheriff said. Standing up, I walked to the front of the cell, my fingers reaching for the steel bars. "Sheriff, don't blame yourself. You did all you could do. If anything, I was the one that should've done things different. Perhaps if I would've, I wouldn't be in this predicament now. But I didn't. I done what I felt was right for me to do. You just done what was right for you to do, that's all.

"I reckon we spend most of our lives making decisions, but I suppose in the end those decisions make us. But the hell of it is, if I had it all to do over again, I'd do it the same way. I hope you would, too, Sheriff."

The sheriff resignedly nodded his head. "I suppose I would. I guess we really can't change who we are deep inside."

"Naw, I guess you're right," I acknowledged. "Now, get that checkerboard out. The best I remember, I owe you about thirty-two cents. I've got every intention of winning that back."

The sheriff lightly chuckled. Seeming relieved of having that off his chest, he went to retrieve the wooden board.

The saloon across the street, which normally went loud and strong until after midnight, on this night seemed subdued and quiet.

I guess the sheriff read my thoughts. "Finch told me that Moss closed the saloon early tonight. The only ones in there were J.B and Bert and a few of their cronies. It seems most of the local people suddenly got picky about who they drank with."

"Better late than never, I suppose."

"Yeah, I guess so," the sheriff replied.

The midnight oil had long been burning before the sheriff wearily stood up and stretched the kinks from his back. "I reckon it's really none of my business," he said as he began returning the checkers to a worn cigar box in which they were kept, "but we do have a Baptist preacher in town if you would like to talk to him."

I smiled. "I appreciate the thought, Sheriff. But I made my peace already. Actually, I made my peace before I ever rode into Clear Fork."

The sheriff nodded. "I'm sleeping in my office tonight. If you need anything, just holler."

"Thanks, Sheriff. I'll do that."

The night was long as I lay awake, my cell shrouded in the silvery glow of the moon. Somewhere off in the distance, a coyote longingly called from the darkness. My thoughts were immediately swept back to my parent's cotton farm in Tennessee.

Even though it was years ago, it seems only yesterday, with the worn, wooden handles of a plow in my hands, I so plainly remember hearing the alluring call of faraway places that had so powerfully beckoned me. It was the enticing call of distant mountains and plush, fertile valleys. It was the soft, but compelling voice of the desert that had so wantonly reached out to me. A desert, seemingly so harsh and dead, yet in reality so very much alive. It was a call so seductive and irresistible that I was left with no choice but to willingly answer.

As I stood staring through the barred window, the stars began to fade, yielding to the inevitable light of a new dawn. I suppose like most men, I have felt the warmth of the sunshine and I have seen dark storm clouds gather. But I always had faith that on a bright tomorrow the sun would shine once more. I now knew that was not the case. My tomorrow had become today.

After being served a breakfast that now sat before me cold and untouched, I pulled my watch from my pocket … nine-thirty. I felt my heart quicken as I watched the second hand continue to skip with each tick.

I stood up as the door opened. Sheriff Brady walked in, followed closely behind by his two deputies. Their faces were sullen and drawn tight. After the cell was opened, I stepped out into the narrow corridor.

Placing my hands behind my back, I felt the cold steel of the handcuffs on my wrists as the sheriff clicked them into place.

"Sheriff, if it's all the same," I said as I looked at the shackles he held in his hands, "I would like to be able to walk up the scaffold like a man."

The sheriff hesitated before bending over and placing the cumbersome shackles on the floor. When he raised up I could see a mist cloud his eyes. "Is there anything else, Chance?" he asked.

"Yes, sir. That mustang I was ridin' was a gift from a friend. I would like it sold with the rest of my belongings and the money sent to my folks in Tennessee. My diary is setting on the cot along with a letter. The letter has their address on it."

"I'll take care of it personally," he said through strained features.

"Thanks," I said as I drew a deep breath. "Finch, take care of yourself." The deputy nodded.

"Sorenson, remember that mirror? You can look at it with your head held high." I saw tears welling before he uncomfortably averted his eyes.

"Sheriff ... I'm ready."

The sun was bright and glaring as the sheriff opened the front door of his office. The morning's air that met us lay unusually heavy and dormant. An enigmatic hush fell over the small crowd that had gathered outside. Stepping from the boardwalk, I followed the sheriff into the dusty street. To the west a small storm was gathering over the desert, giving reason for the moisture-laden air that enveloped the town.

In a vacant lot directly across the street in front of me, a large wooden gallows loomed large and daunting. A temperate breeze from the distant cloud began to sift its way through the street, causing the hangman's noose to gently sway back and forth.

As we walked, a heaviness like I had never known pulled unmercifully at my legs. My breathing became shallow and labored. Upon reaching the base of the gallows, I paused. My eyes followed the ascending steps upward before coming to rest on the knotted rope that hung from a large cross member. Standing near the edge of the platform stood a preacher. He was dressed in black, a bible held before him as he patiently awaited my arrival.

I could feel the sheriff's hand on my arm as he stood silent beside me. Somehow, his light grip felt reassuring and gave me the courage to take that first step … and then the next. I felt my knees weakening as we continued to climb. My footsteps, as well as those of the sheriff and the two deputies, rang loud and hollow on the wooden steps. Stepping up on the platform, I saw a jagged flash of lightning as it was cast from the distant storm clouds. A low rumble of thunder soon followed.

Stepping atop the trap door, I gazed out over the crowd. Most of the faces I saw were strangers, with the exception of J.B. Ross and his son Bert. They stood front and center.

The preacher moved closer to me before he softly spoke. "Son, would you like to pray?"

I shook my head. "Preacher, I reckon I already done all the praying that needed doing."

He solemnly nodded before retreating to the spot where he previously stood.

"Come on, Sheriff!" J.B. called out. "Get this done! Some of us have more important business to tend to than watching some killer swing!"

I stared straight ahead, determined not to give Ross any more satisfaction than he had already taken from me.

Feeling the touch of the sheriff's hand on my shoulder, I glanced over. "Chance, do you have anything you want to say?"

"No, sir," I said as I firmly clinched my jaws. "Just get it over with."

The sheriff was reaching for the noose when I heard a steady drumming. At first I thought it was thunder, until from the far end of the street I saw five riders spurring hard. A cloud of dust was doggedly trailing behind their running horses.

"Hold up, Sheriff!" the man riding a big black horse hollered.

The sheriff was still holding the noose in his hand as the riders slid their horses to a halt at the edge of the perplexed crowd.

"What the hell is this?" J.B. Ross spewed. "Who the hell are you to interfere with justice?"

McCandle's eyes fixed hard on Ross. "I'm U.S. Marshall John McCandle," he said. His eyes held long and hard on Ross before he turned his gaze to Brady. "Sheriff, uncuff your prisoner."

Deputy Sorenson quickly moved behind me. I felt the handcuffs slide open and my hands freed.

Ross was completely beside himself with anger as he began yelling at John McCandle. "You can't do this!"

"Sheriff," McCandle said, "we have proof that everything Chance Tucker said in his testimony was the truth."

"That's a lie!" Ross bellowed. "It's all a blatant lie! That man is guilty of rustling my cattle and murdering three of my men!"

A disgruntled rumbling began building in the crowd as J.B. Ross frantically turned to them. "It's a lie! You can't possibly believe such a thing as that!"

"Ross," McCandle continued, "we have a sworn statement from five of your men saying that not only was you stealing cattle from the Box-T, but that you directly gave the order to kill Tig Jones and Chance Tucker."

"No!" Ross' voice screeched like that of a wounded animal.

I saw Bert Ross's hand flash toward his pistol at his side as John McCandle reached for his.

In the same instant, J.B. turned toward me. "I'll see you in hell, Tucker!" he yelled as he frantically clawed for his gun.

Slamming into Sheriff Brady with my shoulder, I grabbed the pistol from his holster as I knocked him aside. I was bringing the forty-five level as J. B's pistol belched flame. I felt the searing burn of a bullet across my cheek before my own gun bucked in my hand.

As I thumbed back the hammer of the single-action revolver for another shot, I saw J.B. Ross unsteadily sway on his feet. From a small round hole between his eyes, a bright crimson trail of blood began to trickle down his face. His arm slowly lowered to his side before the gun slid from his lifeless fingers. His eyes were grossly wide, as he slumped to his knees before pitching facedown into the dirt.

His son Bert lay dead next to him.

CHAPTER 19

I was standing alone in front of the sheriff's office as I pulled the cinch snug on the mustang. Throwing my saddlebags behind the cantle, I lashed them firmly in place before reaching into my coat and retrieving the black diary from the inside pocket. I paused as I held the tattered book in my hand.

Sheriff Brady and John McCandle came walking out the front door of the office and stood next to me.

Eyeing the diary, Sheriff Brady said, "Well Chance, I guess you ain't quite done writin' in that book after all."

"No, sir. I reckon I'm not," I replied as I carefully wrapped the small black book in an oilskin and placed it in my saddlebags.

"Chance, I wish you would stay," Brady said as he extended his hand. "Clear Fork could sure use a man like you."

Shaking the sheriff's hand, I said, "I appreciate that, Sheriff. But I reckon it's time for me to move on."

McCandle, taking the makings from his shirt pocket, began rolling a smoke. "So, Chance, where are you headed?"

"Oh, I don't know for sure," I replied as I swung into the saddle. "I think I'll head over to Tennessee and see my folks. But I'll probably swing through Santa Fe on the way. There's someone there I really want to see."

McCandle nodded as he struck a match and touched it to the end of the cigarette. "You'll probably be needin' this," he said as he reached into his waistband and handed my pistol to me.

I smiled as I held the Colt forty-five in my hand. The walnut grip felt smooth and comforting.

The sheriff looked confused. "Where did that come from?"

"It's Chance's," McCandle stated with no further explanation.

"I haven't ever seen it before," the sheriff remarked. "He sure didn't have it with him when he turned himself in. How did you end up with it?"

"He seemed to have misplaced it awhile back. I reckon I was just lucky enough to have come across it."

The sheriff furrowed his brow as he shot a skeptical glance between the two of us.

Leaning down from the saddle, I shook the big man's hand. "Thanks, Mister McCandle. Thanks ... for everything."

A smile shown behind his drooping gray mustache. Touching my spurs to the ribs of the mustang, I left town at a lope. I never looked back ... only forward.

Once out on the open prairie, I pulled the mustang to a halt atop a small rise. I could feel the soothing warmth of the early morning sun as it came to rest on my shoulders. The brilliant sky was clear and appeared endless, as it stretched unimpeded from one horizon to the other. The air seemed as pure as any I had ever drawn into my lungs. I sat silent a moment, listening. A soft breeze whispered across the open grassland, carrying with it a faint but alluring call of the yonder.

The mustang, bobbing its head, impatiently pawed at the ground as I reached down and patted its shoulder.

"Let's go, boy," I said as I turned loose the reins.

The mustang ran a hole through the wind as we sped across the open land, chasing the sun. The trailing dust tried to follow, but slowly settled with our passing.

ABOUT THE AUTHOR

ZANE WITH BLACKJACK RITA

Z ane Sterling was raised in Scurry County, Texas, on a farm and ranch owned by his family for three generations. With cotton and cattle being a longtime family tradition, Zane grew to have deep love for old west history.

After graduating from high school, he began his wandering years with an insatiable desire to explore beyond the next horizon. His travels led him to work in the oilfields of West Texas, to being a pit boss in casinos from the Gulf Coast of Mississippi to Reno, Nevada. No matter where he traveled, Zane used every opportunity to quench his thirst for western history.

After years of travel, the intrigue of bright lights and glamour of the corporate world left him empty. Trading in his three-piece suit for reliable work boots and a cowboy hat, he once again turned to those deep roots of his past. Zane began shoeing horses and starting colts with his good friend and well-known horse trainer, Bob Erickson.

With the old west flowing through his veins and a desire to share his stories, Zane began writing and performing Cowboy Poetry in 1998. His poetry has been published in numerous newspapers from California to Texas. One of his most memorable experiences was sharing the stage with one of the best Cowboy Poets in the world, Waddie Mitchell, in Vinton, California, at the longest continuing cowboy poetry gathering in the state.

Striving to once again reach out and touch a distant, gleaming horizon from his childhood dreams, Zane began writing western novels. With the completion of *Debt of Vengeance*, Zane has turned his attention to *Texas Callin'*, the first book in the Brothers of Bull Creek series.

"Having been born into a family steeped in American history and the history of Texas, I feel an obligation to pass along that history. I hope to be remembered as a man who, with pen and paper, was able to crack open a window to the distant past, allowing those with a sense of adventure to be able to walk in those same boot prints as did those before us."